THE JOY DECISION

Rhapsodies for the Afflicted

eos azar

THE JOY DECISION

Rhapsodies for the Afflicted

the kind press

First published by the kind press, 2021

Cover design: Nada Backovic
Internal design: Nicola Matthews, Nikki Jane Design
Internal images: Bliss Inventive
Edited by: Georgia Jordan

Cataloguing-in-Publication entry is available from the National Library Australia.

ISBN: 978-0-6450113-4-0
ISBN: 978-0-6450887-6-2 (ebook)

To Pav –

for everything

and Otis, Birdie and Aristotle –

for igniting inevitable joy within me

CONTENTS

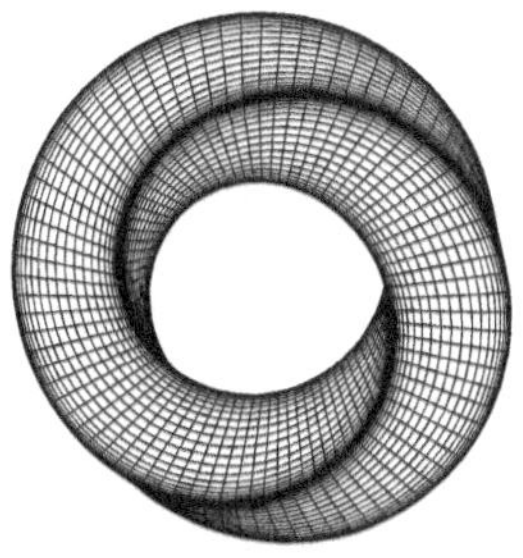

PROLOGUE

The Artist sat for some time, fingertips gripping a brush of glistening crimson. He'd intended to sign his name in the bottom corner, his signature feathery upon canvas, the sigil of his devotion to the piece he'd so dearly tended.

Yet his hubris now yielded to something he'd not felt before. His limbs and body seemed distant to one another. His gut felt empty even though he'd not long ago eaten. The sight of his work did not excite him as it once did, but perplexed him.

Technically, the painting was exquisite. The oils had slid and danced their way into the fibres. Each colour calling the eye to shape and detail that could have been lost to a lesser artist. His hand, strung with proud tendons that had painted every day for months now, fell, soft and hesitant.

The Joy Decision was to be his masterpiece, his magnum

opus. He'd first found the idea for such a gesture flickering within him as he sat one night working on another portrait, the same as the one before it, the same as the one that would follow. *I could be more,* he thought to himself.

Somehow, despite his ambition, he'd become a brush for hire, painting frescos and portraits for the King. *It was barely art,* he'd often think to himself as his inspiration waned and his hands followed the same familiar pattern.

In sittings, the King would look broken and ail. Yet The Artist would cast his brush over canvas in the same way he had for years, not a wrinkle, just the one chin. Power, it would appear, still coursed his veins.

He'd show the King his pieces, as was the custom, and the King's chin would rise a little as his tunic stretched, the chest bulging beneath it. The King would smile in a way that The Artist would wonder if he were perhaps dementing. Then he'd nod to his advisors and shift his ample weight into one leg, turning slowly to walk away.

The Artist would look to his painting, stretching to reconcile the painting before him with the man who had waddled away. He'd sign in crimson, the colour of the court, before advisors handed him his monthly allowance.

The Artist rarely had an audience before, most of his works were condemned to the King's private halls where the ruler would look upon himself as though the frames held a mirror, and he was ten years younger and many pounds lighter. The footmen would pass and offer the slightest of smirks to one another.

The Queen, however, would stand besotted. Her eyes misting as the painting would offer her memories of their courtship. She'd barely seen him in the years since she birthed only daughters and this would tickle her nostalgic senses.

She wanted something big, she said to The Artist one day in the garden. Her arms swanned with the imprint of her dance training as she pointed to the grey walls lining the conservatory.

Something 'ethereal' she said, waving and swirling her hands as though paint dripped from her fingers.

The Artist devoted himself to the garden and the light that seduced its walls. Each day, he'd come and watch as the sun danced upon stormy grey paint.

It was excruciating for his temperament. He'd spent the last thirty years following the same explicit conditions. Yet here he was, feeling quite the dilettante aspiring for 'ethereal'.

The great oak, which had grown since the first king's reign, sat thick outside the conservatory window. Its trunk and branches blocking much of the light, yet at precise moments a sultry glow would peek through the shade. He'd sit each day for months, sketching each hollow between the trunk and wall, the shadows that would dance and the ambrosia beams that would flood the room at twilight.

He worked for a year to capture the perfect deciduous sun and the muses, the Queen and her daughters. Their faces were framed perfectly by the filtered sun, illuminated by innocence and basking in autumnal purity. The youngest plucked flowers from the field, the Queen tended to tapestry—the 'Mater

Eternis' he called her, the eternal mother, as she held her seat as more than a queen, more than the King's wife. The eldest daughters held hands as they danced and silk skirts would flare and wander.

The Queen hosted a party in honour of its completion. Her eyes, and others, she said, required a brilliant final harvest before the light would fade and once more shy into the oak. Guests poured into the conservatory, struck by the depiction that at once delivered honesty, while also brimmed with the immortal.

"You simply must paint *for* me," the nobility urged.

"You must paint *me*," The Baroness said, her voice a heavy treacle that spilled into the garden.

As the rumblings of society became louder, the myth of the picture also became more epic in its retelling. "The verdant picture of fertility touched by the creator Himself," he heard once as he walked through the market. He'd always assumed such things would feel quite wonderful to hear, but here he was, feeling it anchor to him like a lead fetter.

It seemed this was all he could be now. Of miracle and magic.

Her patronage asserted within him a higher ambition. He'd never sought to be seen as anything other than a portrait artist, but the Queen had insisted on gifting him the studio and supplies for him to explore more than the mundane, away from the structured demands of the ageing King. This had to be something impeccable, something pristine. Something *holy*.

He sifted his life for inspiration, for the fulcrum that would animate his greatest offering. He looked to his days, to his lover and his wife. He looked upon his children as they slept, and to the beasts in the field. He'd search in his travels, to the east and the wonderment of stars. He followed snowflakes north to where his breath was held hostage by the tremendous and terrifying glory of the dancing lights.

Nothing would fill his gaping desire. He felt a shape within, a container of vessel that required a specific viscosity to be filled. It demanded a fluidity that would wash through his cells and guide each brushstroke. The timbre echoed of home, but not a home he'd ever lived in.

Until one day, he stood in the market and came upon the poppy man. His cart had been weathered through travel and neglect. His wares obscured to the innocent. To the uninitiated, he was just a ragged old man with a collection of pungent rugs. Yet The Artist had lived a life before this one and knew too well what the poppy man was spruiking.

A violent wave of memory slammed The Artist's mind. He felt himself craving, though he'd dare not indulge.

"Wanna touch the sky?" The poppy man clutched at The Artist's arm with putrid despair, each word stretching upward as though strung by furies.

"No, no, no thank you." The Artist stopped. Ordinarily, he was quite adept at thwarting the advances of peddlers, but this time his past seeped into the present, and shame crawled up his vertebrae.

"Sure you do," the poppy man gleaned, his eyes suspended

somewhere between here and the heavens.

"No!" The Artist yelled, this time staunch in his command. He threw the poppy man's hand from his arm, the peddler's gaunt frame falling backward into the cart, his head softly hitting rotting wood.

The Artist took a few steps back, before being absorbed by the passing crowd. He turned and walked away as swiftly as his disdain would propel him.

I am no longer he, The Artist thought defiantly. His past had, up until now, been the other side of a deep ravine. He'd once taken such a leap from over there with the poppy man, the harlots and degenerates, that he created a schism so irreconcilable amnesia would flood his memories.

Yet the poppy man had shaken him in such a way that bitter memories did resurface. The singular image of a desperate wretch of a man, the perpetual search for shelter and a high.

I am no longer he. Venom pulsed through his veins. He'd looked quite the gentleman, striding through the marketplace with a tangible suspension of class in wisdom. How could such a filthy man violate his day? *How dare he enquire of my proclivities.*

His fury swirled as he continued along the cobbled path. Hawkers called to his empty face, his awareness entirely directed within, at the vast successions of judgements tempered by praise.

He made a decision long ago to never again sit with those that chase the dragons. He'd made a decision to forget all the grimy ways he'd managed to find himself poppy back then, all the stories he'd tell himself and others to find what mattered most.

A joy decision. The words rolled through the back of his head, falling slowly to his tongue where they seemed to stick as though 'I'm important, wait for me'. *A joy decision.* It felt inevitable to him as he allowed the words to slip from his mouth, his eyes glistening with recognition of *that* thing. The thing he had sought for months.

He held the appointment within his cells, each perspective serving a rapturous possibility. Visions sprawled heartily across his mind, with a glory that would rival the masters. He prodded at its placenta, the eternal nourishment of art that was yet to be laboured but offered completion in all sensation.

The Artist felt the unfamiliar grips of a smile spread across his face. He couldn't recall the last time something felt this immense, a fleshy concept, fertile and pious. It breathed in an untempered bliss. It was an entire cosmos of breathtaking and exquisite beauty.

The more he pulled upon threads, the more that was revealed to him. *What do you look like?* he asked.

A verdant canopy, a paradise, a scene of ecstatic bliss rupturing upon the canvas. *My joy decision,* he reminded himself again, his body postured smugly. It'd been such a time that he felt such fervour for a project, and perhaps he'd forgotten how to court such things with grace.

It's a fine life I've made for myself. Dinners in the court drinking from the opulent goblets of royalty. Meandering in the palace grounds. All, he gloated in conclusion, because he'd made the singular decision to commit to *joy*. To cast the beasts of his past and shed his desire for poison. To be happy with just being.

His arrogance waxed further, *this will be a masterpiece*. What an incredible and intentional thing to reflect upon. His own wicked journey and subsequent merriment in life. Pride swelled within him, confirming the project.

As he walked back to the studio, his feet summoned a new pace. Energy flooded his cells in new ways, and his thoughts sparked new connections. *This will be my Eden,* he thought, *and I will be God.*

The Artist opened the studio door, pouring sunlight over dust that had settled but now danced and twinkled in the air. It had been a while since he last visited, and he found on his desk the pensive sketches he'd intended to rouse the muse.

Ripping his pages until they yielded to white, he took the charcoal in his hand and hunched over his bench. He wouldn't sit for this. He couldn't.

It seemed an instant before he'd poured a paradise onto the page. A sumptuous garden, the operatic reprise of heaven on earth. This was something to behold, he realised. The textures were singing, the lines frolicked.

For the next eight months, he devoted himself to the brush. Each stroke a sanctimonious reflection. The more he tethered himself to the visions of joy, the greater his sensitivity to it became. He'd notice the obvious and the obtuse, the subtle, tender and demure.

It hadn't much been his nature to notice much beyond

himself before, having spent great periods of time married to safety. He'd constructed a world merely to serve him, and yet here he was, finding the thrill in unassuming places.

He'd watch joy spring in the beggars and the infirm. The urchins in the street would serve an opera of joy, saturating him in their presence, investing him in their games. He wondered where it all came from, such pure delight, when they were stripped of all that he had found fundamental for his own happiness.

The Artist would move from the streets and the parks back to his studio, longing to convey the brilliance that shone before him. Over thirty years he'd honed his craft to become a savant for royalty. They'd look to him, their ears wide open, drinking his every word on art and its production, its history and methods. Yet this eluded him. To capture the spark that beamed from these tiny children and paint them within his Eden.

One day, as he walked through the piazza he heard the priest shouting and the piercing chorus of the children laughing. They'd managed to get into the bell tower, and flung their tiny bodies to the ropes, setting the bells off in a frenzy. It lacked the holy cadence the priest and brothers were trained in, yet something bright resounded from each toll. Bonggg. Bong, bong. It wasn't merely duty that struck each tone, as it would for the clergy. There was a profound innocence that played at his heart. As the priest shooed the urchins away, the bells rang for a moment more before ebbing silent.

The Artist rolled a coin to the street where they played, it fell gracefully as its diameter rolled and caressed the dust it was to settle in. He'd probably timed it poorly, as the baker had just given them a loaf to share, their shrunken bellies full of crust and crumb.

The eldest picked the coin up, holding it up to the sun as though to test if it were solid. The Artist assumed he would squander it for himself, for later or for the dominion he'd hold tomorrow when their bellies would ache. Instead, he rolled the coin again, watching it in the pregnant moments when it would still and before it would fall. The children took turns, in baited ecstasy, as each had their own attempt to make the coin stand as The Artist had, so thoughtlessly. The air filled with wonder. Laughter spilled from their mouths and into the dusty streets and up to the windows where laundry would hang. The palpable and the rich, screaming, excited, glee-filled vessels of pure joy.

The Artist forced himself to render just one of these divine children on his canvas. There was one, in particular, a small girl whose flesh was not as sunken as the others. She looked somewhat removed from their collective rag and knot existence, but her joy was incredible. Her eyes would beam with a vast curiosity, beyond the meal, beyond the street, beyond the world. He imagined her in his Eden and painted her there. She would dress as all would in his world, proper, yet not condemned to the finery that would stifle her play. He gave her a ball and threaded it to the sky while she gazed in obvious awe, her face amazed by her ability to throw a ball to heaven.

He'd come back every day, in the hope that he could imbue her with sufficient light, with the right light, and capture the luminance she exuded in the street. He was desperate to paint her perfect, to find every grubby mark upon her skin and the dust upon her dress.

He once held up some bread and called to her, "I have something you want."

He'd barely finished his sentence before she clipped back, "You could only imagine what I want," like a young wife scolding her new husband.

You could only imagine what I want. Her words plucked at the hair on his neck as he felt in that moment he could not despise her, nor adore her, more.

One day, he retired from the ambition. He'd spent weeks in earnest and yielded nothing more than a glint in her eye. He felt he'd stretched and exposed every technique he'd ever learnt. He went to the court to see pieces by the masters and still could not find a stroke that would echo what he saw in her.

He buffered his disappointment and inadequacies with an opulent display of archetypal glory. He'd fill his canvas with the typical and the extreme, gods and symbols of joy and prosperity. Zeus, content as he looks upon a new mother, her baby tenderly wrapped in linen and the sun beaming down between heavy clouds. In a private enclave of the garden, a young woman touches fingers with a sprite, an obvious sigil of magic. The canvas would spill with exquisite fruits, falling ripe to a blanket of grass gently swept by the wind. A cool breeze on a warm day, his subjects both human and hero, all blissfully happy to exist in this world.

The canvas sat full for some time. The Artist had intended to go celebrate yet found himself again in the fabric of squalor, the dust on his shoes as rain fell to the earth.

He listened intently to the squealing delight of the urchins. Each marvelling at the puddles filling and the colour of their skin as the dirt washed away. He couldn't identify what he saw. Not from his years of training in art, nor from his intrigue of human spirit. He watched for days as the children would play in their world, immersed in presence and magic and curiosity and joy.

The Artist sat before the canvas, frozen. He could, in all probability, serve this to the museum and they would prop it against the greats. His technique was impeccable, each character thrumming with vitality and movement. The pulse of creation humming in the trees. Three steps back from the painting and one could feel struck, quite strongly, by the poignant reverence for life.

Yet when he looked upon his subjects each one would stare at him with a piercing knowledge. They began to whisper words that hit him as truth. He'd never thought to listen to them before, he never knew he could.

He'd thought if he followed the fibres as every painter does, eyes above nose, above mouth upturned, that was how one painted joy. But they told him more.

In the silence of the night, he watched them. The lamp creating silhouettes and dancing light across the canvas, faces illuminated as the wind hit the flame, like an oracle revealing a higher secret for those willing to undress the logic and submit to mystery.

They'd whisper to him in the nights where he was troubled and sleep evaded him. He'd come down to the studio in his nightdress and slippers just to watch them, to listen to them. A chorus of whispers tormenting him, each speaking over the other so to isolate one and honour its word would prove impossible.

What do you want from me? He asked one night, particularly exhausted and tinged with the mania of countless sleepless nights. Their whispers got louder, though still inaudible in any recognisable sense.

He threatened to sign his name, a desperate and final attempt at closure. He picked up his brush, crimson pigments glistening by lamp light.

Somewhat astounding was the calm that swept him, in a way that only poppy had before. He stood, unencumbered by the network of criticisms within his mind.

He walked through the door and into the dark of night, through the palace gates and into the streets, not waiting for his eyes to adjust. He searched the arteries that led to the centre, discovering the urchins upon the baker's stoop, a bundle of bodies cached for warmth.

Their tender limbs mangled together, their lungs spluttering. Their vulnerabilities here, naked to the world, each harrowing blemish exposed as the wind would lift through their scanty cloth and bite at their muddied skin.

The Artist sat, the insufficiencies of his nightgown and slippers paling in brutal comparison to these unfortunate and forgotten images of bliss. To think he'd iconised them, held them by the canvas with such unrequited reverence. He'd poured devotion into the depiction of these lowly beings, a wondrous explosion swirled his pallet as he endeavoured with every drop of his mortal blood to capture their joy.

He walked back to the studio solemnly. His chest crushing and palpating in the dichotomy of sorrow and sanctity. His heart aching for the little urchins.

How was it they embodied a glow he'd never witnessed before? Not in his own children as they'd play with the children of the court. He had never held such joy. Nor did his magnum opus.

All that he'd intended to achieve, for the technical labour of beauty splashed upon canvas, he'd done that. But within his exploration and attunement to the force he labelled *joy* he'd discovered something more.

Far beyond the theatre where the actors repeated their lines. Far beyond the curated grounds of the palace and the conversations within. There was a tangible difference.

He had happiness. They had joy.

There was something about the darkness that led those urchins to light. He realised his painting, and for the most part, his life, had all been oriented toward the safe, the calculated, the sumptuous arrangement of happiness.

What those children have, that the noble children did not, was an aching chasm of darkness. A departure point for their referential experience of joy. Behind the shining glee he'd tried so hard to capture, was an intimacy with night.

They'd huddled by the baker's door, desperate to siphon any residual heat from the oven. Their only company the dying coughs of their friends. They knew, more than any soldier, the spirit of fortune. And yet come morning when they'd fight the cats and pigeons for the crumbs that fell as customers walked from the bakery and through the square, they knew the world could change. Their antennae broadened to capture any miracle, any possibility.

The Artist looked again at his little urchin girl in the garden, her eyes wide with the juvenile breath of spring. Unfettered awe gripped her mouth and pulled it skyward.

That was what he missed, he thought. Her story.

He began to inspect his other subjects, each missing something he'd never been taught, nor thought to investigate. The story, the feelings, the unconscious chords that would pulse through their bodies. The densities that would stretch and warble as they created an incredible brilliance and contrast for light to beam. In paint, he knew this, yet in experience, he'd been feeble.

There had been times when he'd asked the King about his day, or the Queen about her favourite opera, but their faces always strained the same way, regardless of their words. So, he'd capture what he saw, or what he was told to.

You could only imagine what I want. Her words from the day in the piazza hit his head hard, like a stone thrown by a stranger he'd never identify.

You could only imagine what I want.

The Artist set his painting to the side, confessing to it that he knew nothing. He pulled a new canvas from the stack and prepared it to receive much more than the physical licks of paint that would soon adorn it.

"Now," he said, looking curiously toward his discarded masterpiece, "tell me about *you.*"

AN ACHING DIVINITY

He began his journey in quite the same manner he did anything, by deciding to do, or not to do. He'd been feeling claustrophobic for some time now, sinking in his cesspool of circumstance. He couldn't quite strike the exact note, but he knew that this melange of experiences was guiding him to something quite exquisite.

He'd been sitting at the stoop of the old trading post for much of the morning. The vagabonds had made it quite a place for themselves, and they'd sit and talk about much more than the town and stock and weather. Some of their ideas would sweep him up and set him adrift in wonder. There seemed to be quite a bit more to the world than what his parents would have led him to understand. He found it enticing, to listen and ponder, much to the disgrace of the townsfolk.

It wouldn't be long before they'd be moved along. They used to sit by the stream until the men boarded up the stairs and gave only their wives keys. They'd been getting stirred by the presence of these wanderers watching them. But for this morning, they'd been left in peace.

The Traveller's eye trailed from watching the mouth of

a northern man and upward to the sky. A plume of smoke drifted above the fields and landed plum in his line of sight.

"Murder," one vagabond said. His voice struck the same chord as those who would walk by and spit their insults.

The Traveller dropped his head to one side, noting that this man must be mistaken.

"It's just the old crops," he offered, feeling pleased with himself to share wisdom with those that so freely imparted theirs.

"Yep, murder," the same one said, this time being echoed by others.

"What? How?" The Traveller asked, remembering only that his parents would claim it killed the weeds and prepared the soil for the next crop.

"It sucks the soil. One day, nothing will grow there."

He was received with laughter as he told his father, who gushed that vagabonds knew nothing of soil, and even less of crops. It was madness, and besides, he'd told the boy not to talk to them.

It was then that The Traveller made the strict decision to leave. He knew nothing of the lands he intended to go, only that they weren't *here* and for him, that was good enough.

He stood by the track that led beyond the great dunes and calculated his adventure. Three days and he'd arrive in the big town, and from there he could find some work before he moved farther, crossing the seas and into lands where his tongue would be naked.

His childhood had been remarkably quaint. He shifted through the forest floor in the games he would play with his dog and sometimes his neighbour. He didn't like to say but mostly he preferred to play with his dog, his neighbour would impose rules on him that made the game—his game—quite stifling.

He'd been so free to explore back then, with no expectations on his time and where he was going and what the villagers would think. He could rise at dawn to greet the sun as it twinkled through the foliage and then return at dusk when the radiant glow could swallow his dreams and metabolise them into something ethereal and inevitable.

As he grew, he'd hear the villagers whisper in ways that led his mother to weep, although she'd say it wasn't because of them. He knew he'd mostly been a disappointment to his family, as his brother tended the flock and came home to eat, standing beside his father in stature and morality. He'd mostly felt himself the 'other'.

He'd taught himself to read which was unnecessary and selfish. He'd also sit with the vagabonds and listen to their wild version of living. He'd be captivated by every word, every story, every misty-eyed gesture that would allude to memories beyond description. The Traveller was indeed an anomaly in his village, and it was no secret.

In the confidence of his youth, he felt aware of the necessity of grabbing each part of his loathsome self and holding it beyond their reach. Somewhere, in engaging with these mysteries, he'd learnt that being different was not such a terrible thing, although they would try and excavate his desires and turn him into the parts of themselves that even they did not like.

After his dog had passed, he felt his body becoming too big for the forest. The trees he once climbed would now bend and snap as he pulled his way up their weary limbs. He knew every inch of the floor and had contemplated his path at every branch, each tree imploring him to go, to grow, to expand.

He left the track and moved toward the first great hill, knowing that all things were about to change. His eyes widened to capture the panorama, a world unbound by trees on the periphery, bare land surrounding him in every direction. It felt so wonderfully big here, so open and expansive. He could breathe, the dry air filling his lungs in crevices that had not received oxygen since his first, virgin breath.

The Traveller had not planned on sitting to eat so soon in his journey, but something about this immaculate space begged him to absorb all that he could while he was here—to marry the nourishment of his eyes with that in his belly. He pulled from his bag a neat little parcel of olives and nuts, the bitter fruit reminding him of the place he had left behind.

As he swallowed the last few morsels, he realised something he'd never before pondered in his village. *I know nothing.* While he had the stories of some that had said they'd been beyond, he never knew what was fiction and what was true. In the maps that he'd seen when others dared to dream, how could he know they were real? His eyes had rarely proven false, yet in books, there was no way to test and live the words and hold memories that guide your feet.

I know nothing. He smiled. There was something wildly liberating about that notion. That he could submit to the weather or the trail or the people that he'd meet. That each day could be an unexpected delight of miracles that would land at his feet, and he could simply choose yes or no. There was no plan, no strictures, no casing to hold him back. That here, on his journey, knowing *nothing* gave him the overwhelming freedom to ask and receive.

The Traveller had, up until the moment he left his home and much to the further disappointment of his mother, not been a boy of faith. He wouldn't stoop at the rocks in the field as he began each day as his father and brother did. He wouldn't kneel before bed to wish something powerful to change something powerless. He'd always felt an impending sense of responsibility to take such things upon himself or settle into acceptance.

But now, knowing *nothing*, he felt it quite a suitable time to entertain such a force. *If I know nothing, then all that I am made of, the flesh that fills my skin, that must come from something. And that something must, whether conscious or not, know the equations that fuel the universe, both the mundane and the miracle. That something that left the grasshopper on the leaf in the forest in the same perfect shade of green, and the something that brought rain to the crops.* He knew nothing, he thought, even though he knew *something* was there. What that something was, he didn't know.

He decided to make a deal with something. Not a prayer

or wish for anything supernatural, just a deal that he believed would serve each fairly. *Something*, he asked, *as you deposit the rain on the field, may you also deposit the world at my feet? So that I may grow as does the wheat, so that I may move to greatness as does the seed to the stalk?*

He thought, well, at least it seemed to the unknowing, that growth appeared to be the language of the universe. From a young boy who knew nothing, it would not be too much of a thing to ask something.

The Traveller stood, fuelled by the vibrancy of his request. While he still knew nothing, and, had nothing to confirm his words had been received, something welled within. A smile crawled up both sides of his face as he was flooded with a feeling he'd never quite understood. Somewhere within, he held a repository of information propelling him toward *faith*. He'd never managed to fathom it before, because mostly what the villagers called faith he believed was more like control, wish-pulling every outward circumstance into a warped narrative—*God, I don't like this, make it better.*

But he felt something more immense than that which *they* called faith. That the universe was programmed toward expansion, and that no matter what, he would expand. Talking with the vagabonds had proven so, even in the dire moments, they'd still find cause to laugh. Standing amongst the trees he saw the scars upon their trunks and knew that they would grow regardless.

The infinite, that *something*, seemed more than willing to

offer growth, and as it could create stars and valleys and simple little grasshoppers, he thought it best to trust its blessings and follies. *Faith*, he mused. *Fascinating.*

He crossed down into the valley and through the little stream that served the base of the mountain. The water was still warm from the summer as it trickled over his feet, and tiny fish swam around him. He stood and watched them for a while, wondering what it was they were doing as they darted from one direction to the other. He pulled his feet through the water and onto the bank where he sat on a rock and re-tied his shoes.

The mountain was obviously a home for many more creatures than he'd yet encountered. He could hear each burrowing and slithering as he walked nearer to the thickened scrub. Each sound a canvas upon which to paint his fear or joy. There were many stories, back in the village, of what lived upon the mountain. He'd never much listened to them because they were always lined with terror and seemed to lack the wonderment of the stories to which he liked to listen.

As the morning bled into noon, his breath and limbs surrendered to a pace that thrummed with the heartbeat of the mountain. Overgrown thicket would appear on the exhale, a rock would appear as he strode forward. There was a sublime resonance to him, pulsing his life within the life of the mountain.

Somewhere amidst the afternoon sun, a chill began to swirl around his chest. The air felt different up here, breathing was different. The little trees had thinned out so that all that remained were the mighty old pines and the ambitious saplings that hoped to live through winter. One small branch reached out to him and grabbed his shirt, snagging itself to a thread. He freed himself from its grasp and noticed a spot of blood had revealed itself near his rib.

His legs seemed to move through the vines, each desperate to trip or trap him. He found himself dragging his toes higher as the tendrils of each branch snared his socks. He stopped, and reached for his water flask, surveying the scrub before him. His eyes followed a length of vine that wrapped itself around trees for most of the length of the ridge. He found himself mesmerised, watching it coil itself around trunks and tender shoots. It was as though it were saying 'do not proceed', its barbs spiny reminders of a hostile nature.

He stepped now with greater caution as the soil yielded to rock. He'd follow the waterline, where the summer deluge would course its way to the stream and minimise all obstacles. In the shade he noticed lichen growing on the rocks, his fingertips sensing this living entity sharing secrets. *Go there*, it whispered, gesturing deep within The Traveller's body to move from his current course and up across the ridge.

Something, he thought, moving as the lichen willed. The brilliant sense to change course not native to his thought—it must be *something*.

His fingers now steamed with the pace he employed. He clawed and gripped his way upward, sideward, over the fallen trees and to the shadowed side of the mountain. It was much cooler here, he thought, wondering if his single blanket would serve him into the night.

He was close to the top of the mountain and could smell the air once again changing. His hands were burning but a crag rose before him that demanded he climb further. He looked behind him, hoping for another trail that he'd missed, but as rocks fell beneath him, he realised he was standing atop a sheer cliff.

He rubbed his hands against his shirt, hoping the change of texture would be a reprieve to his tingling tips. Summoning his breath to lift him, he inhaled before reaching for the shelf as his legs swayed underneath.

As he pulled himself up, the faint wisps of smoke greeted his lungs. He was far too focused on not slipping to question where it was coming from, as his arms wearied knowing the end was near.

He managed to find a small indent where his toes became fixed, and for a moment caught his breath before questioned his reasoning for listening to lichen. Below him, the wind swirled and howled as it was pushed from the side of the mountain into this hollow. If he fell, his bones would be crushed as his body slammed to the ground. He'd die, and if not, he'd be lame.

Trust. The word would circulate his brain. Trust, he thought, as the blood swam back through his arms. Faith will guide me, trust will anchor me.

He realised that was what they—the people claiming to be of strong faith in his village—missed. They readily believed in the creating force of the universe, that something bigger than them, wiser than them, more loving than them, had a power that resulted in their existence, but when they were challenged, they had no trust. They'd cling to their faith but dial into the creator begging for change when all was beyond their control.

He heard a branch snap somewhere above him, as he tried to calculate how far he had to go. The cliff seemed to now be above him so entirely that it jutted outward, and he could see barely inches above himself. More branches were snapping, and the rhythmic chorus of crushing leaves sounded like footsteps. A goat? He thought, knowing if anything were to be up this high, it must be a beast.

He pulled himself up the next ledge, delicately resting his elbows as he prepared to hoist himself up further. As he caught his breath, he heard the footsteps right by his ear, and tiny, gnarled toes fell beside his nose. He craned his neck to look up, but momentum pulled at his spine, so the best he could do was tilt his head a little to the side.

"Hello," said a small, old woman with her hair falling from its chignon. She reached her frail arm to him, and with might beyond her frame pulled him to the mountaintop.

"Hello," said The Traveller, puddling his bones before her feet. His head, resting in his arms and his eyes taking a moment to acclimate to the view. It was cold up there as the tender fall of snowflakes gathered before his face. His breathing began to settle back into its usual, rhythmic exchange, and as it did his breath was cut short by an acrid wall of smoke.

"Come," the old woman whispered so softly, he'd wondered at all if she intended it for him. She stepped lightly toward a small trail that traced the side of the mountain, before following it around to a cave with cloth and branches covering the entry. The boy at this time was walking so weary that she pulled him inward, the cave glowing with the light of a fire.

Had it not been for his near-collapse into the chasm beneath, he would not have fallen to the floor so easily, but something within had beckoned him to rest, to take this moment to shut his eyes and allow the nether cells of his being to process his awe.

It was warm by the fire, and he fell into a deep sleep.

When he woke, it was morning. The old lady had gone but he could see through the opening that snow still fell. Strange, he thought, as winter was still some months away, although he knew on the mountain that snow did last longer, it could be seen well into spring and sometimes the earliest parts of summer. He walked out from the warmth by the fire and into the breaking rays of dawn. It wasn't cold, he realised. The air did have a frigid tint, but not so much that he went back for his blanket.

As his eyes adjusted to the waxing sun, and as snow fell upon his arm, he realised it didn't melt. He picked a flake between his thumb and finger before it crumbled into powdery ash.

"Big fire," the old woman said, once again her voice so low he had to take an extra second to understand. She pointed across the valleys to the rising sun, and through the violet sky he could make out the thick tendrils of smoke swirling through the foothills.

He took a moment to gather his bearings, looking to the sun and then the stars that still dotted the far horizon, then to the mountain and the valley. At once he was struck by the understanding that this was his home—his forest ablaze. A guttural cry came from within, not words, not tears, but the escaping madness of confusion and disbelief and despair and agony. His boyhood, the uninitiated man, and his naive connection to feelings still obvious with each excruciating breath. He'd not yet learnt to temper these emotions, as the other men did. It was why he was sent to tend to the market and not work the crops with the men and their scythes.

He sat down, eyes glazing as profane thoughts erupted in his head. *You did this,* he told himself. *You wanted to leave the past behind, you killed it.* He had so wished to set off for this adventure, and even though the thought of returning had never quite swallowed him, he didn't question the mortality of the place he loved most. "Why would this happen," he begged to the sky. "Why would this be?"

The old woman whispered beside him, and he steadied his stammers to make out her words. She seemed oblivious to his presence now though, and he realised she spoke in the northern tongue. She turned to him and again spoke words that he knew.

"Aching divinity," she gestured to the smoke amassed by the horizon.

He focused his ears on her mouth, taking time to dissect each syllable and recognise it in context.

"Sorry ma'am, a what?"

"An aching divinity," she said, slower this time, yet still greatly inaudible and desperate for clarity.

A truth fell somewhere in his gut, resonant with the knowledge he once knew but had deposited elsewhere. He vaguely remembered leaving said knowledge in the garden as a child, knowing there would be a time that the ephemeral would once again be triumphed by the cosmic.

"Aching divinity," he rolled off his tongue. He'd never said nor heard those words before, but there was the precise tone of truth within that seemed to unlock his duelling emotions. He swung the words through his mind, a pendulum moving left then right. Each moment it would strike a deeper knowing, a visceral connection rippling through his trembling body and to the ethereal realms he'd so often sojourned.

His mind, feeble in articulation, came to consider it thus: the intentional creation of one's best life, and the parallel destruction as a consequence.

"Did I do this?" He needed confirmation. He needed to know that his selfish foray into the future had not obliterated his past.

"You moved the energy," she whispered, before turning and moving back to the cave, speaking again in her own language and with no obvious intention of an audience.

He howled again, feeling great pain. What was he to do? Were they fighting the fire? He thought of his father and his most responsible brother, thinking without a doubt, they would be there with buckets dousing its flames. He needed to do something, to be back there, to help, to fix. Though he knew that even if he landed upon the front of the battle, he'd be made to ring the bell and then passed to the mothers who would tend to the children.

Helpless, reckless, a searing collection of terror and guilt. He moved back to the cave and lay down on his blanket, overwhelmed by the contradictions. How could something so good, result in something so bad?

The old woman was whispering again, and it took him some time to realise she'd moved back to speaking to him.

"Were you to return?" she asked in such a slow drawl it commanded him to think throughout all of the ages, and not just reply in reaction to his pain.

He envisaged his adventure, the travels he would take from land to land, the life he would live upon the sea and into the deserts and the mountains further north. He imagined meeting great people, who would too think him great. He would witness wondrous things and be at the helm of innovation.

He did not, however, think of returning to his home. And if he tried to stuff that concept into the vessel of wondrous things, it'd bleed into them and tarnish their beauty.

"No," he replied, feeling defeated in his attempts to justify his hurt.

"Sometimes," the lady whispered, this time so quietly he was forced to move forward, sensing catharsis in her words, "overwhelming pain is actually overwhelming joy."

He sat back, denying the proposal. He thought to the woman, who lived in a cave and obviously had no sense of attachment to things of her past. This couldn't be so, he thought, offended by her proposal. *That I'm happy this happened? Not at all.* His heart broke thinking of the trees he would climb, and the birds that would nest and the lizards catching the last drops of sun before night collapsed overhead.

He was broken, not in joy. He couldn't fathom such a concept. That this was the joy? He thought back to his earliest memories, he and his dog playing with the sticks that would fall from the trees, his mother calling to him as a child and his ears oblivious to all but play. He'd climb and wonder and dance by the pond, swirling a stick through the water and watching the fish disperse. He'd call to the birds, learning their warbles and forcing his voice to be shrill. As he grew older he'd take refuge here, under the canopy of bliss that would tether him from the disdain the villagers would spit at him.

He'd breathe the air and fill his lungs with the purity of creation, knowing that this was the exalted hand of reality, not that which they claimed in the market. He'd sit, listening to the leaves falling as the sun tracked lower, watching the green turn to red, and orange, and then the crisp and fragile browns. He'd sit in the silence of winter, listening to a vast and inescapable chorus of emptiness, waiting for the first holy buds to appear and whet his appetite for play.

He'd wait until he wanted no more for the remnants of winter to slide into spring. He'd cherish this moment, where the earth was a womb, ripe for the gentle inseminates of sun and seed and the sprouting wilderness of spring.

He'd remember the first time he'd slept there, not willing to come home as his father had shaken in fury when he'd dropped the scythe and wailed amongst the men. The comfort of the fir, a pillow much like his at home, but warmer and with the rapturous thrum of eternity. He'd taken a vagabond there when the market was not safe from the scorn of society and the stones they would cast. This man, ragged and beaten, stilled by the immense cathedral of beauty behind the first few trees, his eyes misty until they flooded with grace and the recognition of the creator in full display. They sat together with no words, just the shared exchange of awe for this exquisite bliss that straddled the bitter village.

He thought of his final days when he knew he'd be leaving but had not yet told his parents, as he sat under the jasmine that saturated the air with its perfume and glory. He talked to the bark upon its crooked trunk, seeking counsel and exploring possibilities. The audience of the forest, the soil teeming with tiny life, the leaves that would collapse into the earth, the sapling and the tree, the bird and the squirrel all listening unconditional. They'd remind him that beyond the glare and poison tongues, was always the cradle in the woods. He'd barely be able to sit, in those final days, as excitement gripped him, and his magic would rise closer to that of the forest.

Joy, he thought. Such joy. He'd never thought in such entirety of the forest and its pulse that nourished him when the world was sterile. He'd never before thought of it and the way it shaped him in the years when the world would call him names. The wisps of joy would ripple through the trees, a visible ribbon of laughter swirling amongst the mid-morning mist.

Overwhelming joy, he thought as he wept in reverence. How could he hold such joy, and is that all that pain really was, unrecognised joy?

His body pined to be there, to be fixing it, fighting it. His cells each longing for his memories to be pristine, not charred and crumbling. Was that all he was? His mind now sifted through the nature of memories and wondering why they held him captive here. He could return, he thought, and nurture those memories, or he could step forward, and make new ones, greater ones.

He stood, the cave which last night felt unbounded now felt very small. He walked toward the woman, who now sat with a blanket over her knees.

"Thank you," he said, taking her hand in his and pressing his lips to the calloused and fragile skin.

She shut her eyes for a moment, before bowing her head to his. There was something in the silence that eclipsed the norm of formal farewells, a reverence for that greater than the mundane. For the knowing beyond knowing.

He stepped back to the cave entry, looking now at the full light of morning, smoke billowing and filling the sky as the ashes fell around him. He knew not how to reconcile this, be it pain or joy, but he knew it was a part of the process. Of trust stacking upon faith. He dared not beg to change it, though memory clawed at his heart.

He turned his back to the valley, pausing for a moment to shunt his understanding of reality. From this, he thought, he could journey to greater memories, to a greater adventure, the ache etching out space in his heart for greater joy.

He thought of the stars and the words of the vagabonds. They said that we were made when the stars would war and debris fell to the earth—that even the universe exploded so that it could find itself.

"Big boom," the oldest vagabond had said, "make man."

✦ SYRUP HIPS ✦

The Dancer needed no name. The spectacular energy that fuelled her sanguine limbs would announce itself before her arrival. She used to dance for The King, though she'd not seen him since he set her free. One night, she came upon his camp and men appeared around her, in absolute awe. She had an aura, a raw and primal shakti pulsing through her, around her. They'd been mesmerised, following her from the outer posts of the camp and drawn to follow her as she walked toward his tent.

She smelled of perfume the men had never smelled before, sacred oils from the east the holies would share. The wind would cradle myrrh, rose, and frankincense in its grip, stroking upon noses announcing her nearby. She'd been here before, many years ago, and knew her way to his tent. Had she forgotten, though, it would matter not as she'd look to the sky and stars would appear that others couldn't see. The shooting, raining stars would mark her path.

Her hair was black and hung long to her waist. It was wild, not like the hair of the courtesans The King liked to keep, but the silks she wore were more than peasants could afford.

She'd danced for the general too, and for the merchant

who gifted her silk of every colour: crimson, gold and the richest violets. She'd danced at inns and palaces, she'd danced in the wild and the crisp nights in the desert. She'd seen the world. She'd seen dynasties fade and women rule. She'd been a witness to all with her eyes, and yet she'd not changed. Still possessed by the immense power, the echoing base note of the universe that compelled her to move evermore.

On this night, The King knew she'd soon appear. The stench of horses had seemed to dissipate at twilight, and jasmine drifted in with the easterly wind.

"She's here," the guard announced at his doorway. The King sat, relishing the news he thought he'd never hear. He'd owned her once. He'd been so taken with her, this celestial and radiant beauty that breathed the air of Aphrodite. He owned all things and believed she too, would be one of those things. Her skin was not like that of his courtesans, her eyes were fire and her blood magnetic.

The King never commiserated a loss, every moment looking forward. And yet The Dancer beckoned him so. He'd often spent his nights yearning for her skin, desperate to touch that which he had never touched. She'd been born of gods, he knew this. As she danced before him those years ago, he'd been paralysed by the electricity filling the palace. He'd fought battles and never been frozen so.

But The Dancer pulsed the same light that sparked creation. She would fill his loins such that he, The King, sat impotently. He couldn't reach for her, his jaw hanging slack and his breath burrowed a course deeper than even his first gasp as a baby.

She couldn't be owned, this creature of the divine. She was primal and she was light. Storms would pass before her, splitting clouds in two as she walked beneath. A deciduous and unfurling expression of femininity, tempered with the heralded bolt of heavenly strength.

They'd whisper, the courtesans and the village women. Even the men that could not own her would tête-à-tête when they felt the discord of desire and destiny. They had not the language, verbal or unspoken to lure her. Nor to hold her captive, as did The King, which would sterilise that which was sumptuous. Her dance became pathetic, her eyes drowned and the air soured.

She longed for the great expanse of sky that bathed her cells in glory. She'd bask, alone at night, each thought entwined with the love and joy that God intended. She'd roam, her womb full of magic and the essence of creation, to the next camp or village, the port or castle where she would share her intimate and holy expression. She'd be fuelled in perpetuity by the marriage of dance and fire-lit breath sent by gods above.

The King would release her, the only thing he'd yet to conquer. Set his darling thing free in the field with the goats, their bells thrumming their song through her veins, each intensifying and reviving as The Dancer awakened. The air once more stood still.

And yet, here she was, back again.

The King looked back, broken from his thought by his son

stirring.

"You still awake?" asked The Queen, her nightgown falling from her shoulder as The Prince latched to her breast.

"Won't be long," he replied and left the tent. His men were transfixed by the atmosphere, the heavy and pregnant night alive with enchantment. It felt like this before battle, warriors concurred. But here is not hostile.

The liminal address between the cosmic and the mundane seemed to be pulsing, throbbing with connectivity. Gods would sit upon the bridge, breathing their eternal breath before her. The rapturous wind would beat at their skin, their nerves tingling with charge. Before battle they'd say, "Gods would rain their will upon us. Now they rain glory upon us."

She was an omen, an auspicious gift of immortal bliss. When she danced, enemies dissolved, they'd sheath their weapons and kneel to pray. This immortal, this fertile, beaming woman of the universe would sway syrup hips, the sides of her bellied skin peeking smugly from slipped silk. Her undulating shoulders were sensuous and driving, her eyes wide like the dying.

She'd set a flame to their hearts that would warble the tender song of love.

She never knew why she travelled, the winds drifting her to all corners, her body animated by the waves of creation. She'd find herself crossing seas, and atop mountains where men had not been. Her cells absorbing the nourishment of nature and elements, her dance becoming increasingly organic, limbs in the wind as a tree, heart ablaze in fire, body undulating as the ocean.

Why did she return to The King after all these years? She'd not wondered why. The same cosmic seed that propelled her forward in marvel graced her now. That her shakti flame was to be extinguished never crossed her mind.

The drums had been pounding for some minutes now, as she floated closer to The King's tent, each step a levitating embrace of form and fantasy. The men would watch her, this woman that stopped The King, and the throbbing pulse of her movement attuning to their hearts beating wild.

By the fire, she took some wine. She raised the chalice above her head in a sanctimonious offering to the gods. Eyes closed and invoking all men to do the same, The King watched on as this woman commanded his men to embrace the gods that they'd not known.

The Dancer took the chalice and then poured, in a delightful ceremony, the ruby wine in a great circle around her body, spinning as her silk skirts spiralled and fanned like the flames beside her. *Here*, she symbolically demanded, *is my stage. Touch me not. Do not approach. The gods live here.*

"Dancer!" The King called, his voice booming into the night, searching for a place to rest in the desert air. "The Queen and my children sleep here, take some bread and fruit and move on by morning."

The dancer froze, she recognised him only as the man that held her captive and stole her song, but in his voice, she heard something completely new. There was something in the way he said 'my children' that echoed the divinity she inhaled, the magic and enormity of besotted reverence that laced his speech.

She'd never been asked to stop, nor move on before. Few men could summon the strength to address her, and yet here he stood, the man she'd once thought impotent with his fine robes and bitten tongue. He'd never before found the lingual dexterity to even utter a greeting, and tonight he offers a command.

The children had been thrust so deeply into the night, with such authority, the scope of his chest reaching beyond the material. His heart, she felt, had burst open with the intimate introduction of these little beings. It was they, the children, that gave him the power to prime the words.

His men looked about bewildered. She was the omen. The Dancer was the auspicious one, why did The King wish her gone? They stood examining the vacuum between. The King and the mystic. Each steeped in sacred duty, her to receive from the heavens and bring beauty upon earth, he to receive from the people in the name of all that is holy.

Her ears rung violently with the intrusion. Suddenly her feet, naked to the desert sands, began to itch from the dust underneath. She felt exposed and raw. She'd not recognise the sensation, perhaps it was what others called rejection.

The King had hardly meant it but wrapped around the majestic love for his children was the subtle remnants of diffused ego. He broke apart when he set her free. When he realised her magic existed not for him to own. Unlike anything else in his life, he'd offered her the world and yet she faded within it. Her dance became mechanical, contrived, a lamenting chorus of ache and yearning.

That was what had her unravelled. She'd only spoken the divine languages of grace, and joy, and glory, and love and freedom, and here he was, intimating this sacred word with the love for his children, and yet attached was a virus of broken ego, the man rejected and wounds throbbing. She'd readily accepted his love, his appreciation of the enduring mysteries of creation, the humility of parenthood in awe of God and all possibility, and yet as her heart rippled with the resonant vibration of oneness, she found herself exiled.

He turned with ceremony and strode back to his tent. She was left standing, barren, null of all expression and vitality. The spirit that danced through her veins was now gone, and her chest crushed inward.

Her bare feet stroked the desert earth, residual sands lingering upon her ankles, catching and casting the light from the fire. The bells that once chimed against her delicate ankles now clamoured delinquent. Her body once sauntered in rhythm with creation, her hips simmering in symphony. But now her neck fell sallow and her legs were heavy. She dragged clumsy through the night.

She could hear the rising outrage of the soldiers, dissent pounding in their chests for the interruption to God's tiny gift for them. The Dancer had, and would, evermore shimmy in the essence of angels for them. They'd taste the air, feel the wind sing with her approach. And for some madness of fractured ego, The King had sent her away.

She continued through the night, beyond the roar of the fire and the flames of the soldiers' torches. She walked restlessly as never before. Her feet hurt, her ears stung with The King's words, her heart ripped from its gentle existence of freedom and the slipstream of dance. The air was cavernous with her drifting, meandering thoughts. The voice seemed slighter than that she'd ever heard before, an interior monologue presented in stereo, summoned its direction through her being, a whispering giant imploring her to seek more.

My children; each letter spilling from the reverberating cavern between her ears and landing in her womb, forcing its magnetic girdle deeper and stronger, sparking a longing she'd never felt before.

All this time she'd drifted through Earth as through a drop from heaven, she'd not concerned herself with material sensibilities, nor fussed over satiating primal urges. Her all had provided for her, and yet now she felt immensely neglected. The gaping desire rising 'til she could barely breathe.

My children. Had he, The King, seeded her with an unwilling desire? Or had this always been there, now ripe for the words to land and seat her amongst those that yearn?

As the night broke for the dawn, her eyes welled, and kohl dripped to her wrists. She'd not realised she held her hands before her, a cup before her chest in a begging gesture of surrender to her all. As the kohl coursed its way through the lines of her palms, the word 'harlot' broke forth.

"Harlot", the word had never landed upon her so fiercely. Had she heard it in her past? "Harlot," a man's voice, thick and authoritative, a general perhaps, lined her ears and connected a memory.

"Harlot." It started as a whisper and soon become a roar. The words would play for months, as she left the fire and the wild men and their leering and cajoling. She'd not noticed before, how tawdry it'd all been. She'd felt irrepressibly enlivened before, each dance a sermon on living through spirit, and yet now cells in her brain stood to attention vying for acknowledgment.

"Harlot." The words ripping through her mind, each syllable tainted with disgust and disdain. "Har-lot." Memories danced like fireflies though there'd been no memories before. Mercenaries and more seasoned soldiers, The King's guards, all seemed to have at some time been stretched from their mouths.

"Harlot." As she walked past the caravans and women tending to camels the words would spit from their mouths.

Could it be? Her fire, her sauntering ignition of energy and dance and the wild edge of skirts, this is what kept her alone in her journey?

As the desert yielded to hills, an Ibex stood before her. Its nostrils flared and exhaled long. The Dancer had hardly thought its lungs could be so great, to exhale for such a time.

"I remember you," said the Ibex. "But not you," he cocked his head sideward, observing with greater detail than before, as though to pinch upon the change.

The Dancer stood, privy to such examination. She'd felt the surges of rejection gripping her waist since the King brushed her into the night, to capture the gaze of this beast in the day seemed a sweet reprieve.

"You hunger," he concluded, tilting his head gently upward to display the full glory of his horns, each ridge seemingly etched in precision.

"Yes Sir, I need linen," The Dancer replied, bypassing the flame within and instead fanning her shame.

"You hunger for linen?" The Ibex questioned, not understanding this woman that had once danced in thunder.

"The wind bites at my skin," she answered, her nerve endings now timid from the swirling mist of inadequacy.

"There's a line beyond that ridge, linen billows upon it," the Ibex recalls disappointedly. He knows there is more, he knows this woman that used to feed her soul with the nectar of heaven. She was once whole, and holy, but now her heart path had been cordoned and the sprinkling thoughts of a broken spirit became her guide.

If I can cover my limbs, the men would think me decent. Then I could fall in love and bear children thus.

The Ibex moved to the side of the path, before jumping to a higher peak. He threw his head in the direction of the ridge and watched her sadly. He wanted to tell her to climb the mountain she must go up yet knew that she'd only discover that after following the tenuous stream to its depths.

The Dancer arrived at the little hut, to see smoke beckoning her from the chimney, its tendrils swirling and wrapping its way around the pine on the hill. The wind beat violently at the linen on the line, the grey and sullied threads stiff from the rain that had poured upon them earlier in the day. An old woman walked out, nodding and nattering in an unknown dialect.

The old woman slid The Dancer's silk between her thumb and forefinger, delighting in the rubied slip. She looked confused, pointing to the linen on the line. The Dancer nodded, indicating the silk and its limitations in keeping her warm, and mocked shivers. The old woman shrugged, accepting that this young dear thing walked a path carved so deep only ravens may change it.

"What is it dear?" the old woman asked, as The Dancer sat in the hut, wrapped in clumsy linen intended for the shepherd, sipping tea coyly.

"My legs are weak and my belly aches, I so need bread." The Dancer clutched her abdomen in anguish.

If I can fill my limbs, the men would think me womanly. Then I could fall in love and bear children thus.

The old woman, tempered by the dancers longing, showed her the way to the village. She wanted to tell the dancer to hold onto her silk, for when the days are warmer, but she knew the dancer would only see its value once it was gone.

The Dancer walked to the peak, before setting off on the stone-lined path down the hill. The air had changed again, sea mist struck her face, the ocean she'd not seen in sixteen years. She felt far from where she'd been last time she followed the ribbons of light here. It was all dark now, the sun was high and yet clouds filled the sky bitterly.

As she made her way around the curving headland, the

smell of bread drew her downward, the path making way for stacked boulders she'd slip on the lichen grazing her knee. Threads of her linen now unravelled behind her, a thin line suggesting a path for her return.

The Baker froze. He remembered The Dancer well; he'd thrown roses at her wild body last time he saw her. That was long ago now, and although her eyes had dimmed and the bells on her ankles sung no more, he knew it was her. He clapped his hands before his face, pressing them to his lips in a delicate gesture of glee and reverence.

"Dancer!" he sung in his native tongue, the nature of his language was to sound like music no matter the word or intention. "How can I serve you?"

The Dancer knew too few words to understand and pointed to the bread.

"Of course!" He tapped at several loaves, listening diligently to the timbre to suggest perfection. He passed The Dancer bread as a group of women approached the oven. The Dancer looked at these women, noting their long skirts, the high collars and lace. Upon their feet, she saw boots with heels, and each step commanded attention with its defined rap.

The Dancer finished her bread, the smattering of curd barely touching her taste buds as she thought only of the shoes.

If I could cover my feet, the men would listen to me. Then I could fall in love and bear children thus.

The Dancer did not respond to The Baker as he gestured

wine, tea, shisha. His hospitality, his longing to adore her, melted into the air between them. In her mind she was inadequate. No man could want her like this.

"My feet are blistered," she told The Baker, who offered her salve. She turned away, thanking him for the bread before she followed the road to the shoemaker.

The Baker wanted to tell The Dancer not to lose her bells—her music—but he knew that in losing one song she shall one day find another.

The Dancer walked through the market, her feet stumbling on cobblestones, wet from apple tea that had spilled from its cart. The smell of incense and oils, the clamouring chatter of chickens and bartering crowds, the crash of disused pots falling to the stone walkway, all calling her into heightened fragility. Her nerves were ablaze with each interruption.

As she approached The Shoemaker, he shooed away the young man that had sat before him playing dice. His gaze fell to the bells on her feet, and his eyes burst with light. Gold, he thought, and he traced the delicate weave of filament that entwined her ankles.

The Dancer pointed to the soft leather behind him and then to her feet. She knew he'd been disgusted by her naked toes standing in the dust, his glare breaking through the flesh and well into her bones. He'd not stop staring since she got there.

"Twenty coins," he rapped, looking at her face now to see if the gold upon her ankles was the extent of her riches.

"I've not any coin," said The Dancer. The Shoemaker's

crawling smile expanded over his face.

"What of these?" he shouted, pointing to the bells and being open to barter or merely accept just one of the exquisite strings.

"Oh, okay," she said, her hands trembling and heart tender as she passed the solemn remnant of her glory into the eager hands of greed.

The Dancer sat, waiting in reverberating awe as The Shoemaker stitched her boots. Her head felt somewhat housed in a vacuum now, sounds evaporating from around her, the bazaar aromas starved of air, time-compressed. This final parting struck her as she took her first moments to collect herself since The King's dismissal. Barely ten days ago, she'd not searched for much more than what the gods deposited on her journey. Now, her yearnings compelled her to unravel all that she'd known.

She was startled by the tender tugging upon her linen. A thread had fallen loose and wound its way around the marketplace, a goat had found the thread and bleated wildly, curiously, infinitely questioning the choices of The Dancer. For the King, thought the goat, you have lost your all.

As the goat pried its head from the snare of linen, The Baker lifted a knot from its horn. He'd followed the flax trail through the market, savouring the memory of The Dancer in her glory. His chest begged to protect her, to provide the world so he could once again stand, heart arresting, in the full expression of her divinity.

The Shoemaker handed The Dancer her boots before his

eyes fell back to the gleaming bells, his cloth polishing the yoke in dear reverence, his smile encroaching his ears so rapidly that the market chorus muffled. She slid them upon her feet, the soft leather cradling her broken skin and beckoning her to walk with an intimate purpose like the women she'd seen before. This, she now believed, will make me appropriate to wed.

The Dancer walked through the markets, her feet silent and her ankles timid within the boots. The heels had been much higher than the sandals she once wore, her legs stiffened and slipped one after the other and she fell to the sounds of music playing and women laughing.

As she stepped beyond the hawkers and their carts, dozens of young women danced and sung. Their hands grabbing one another before they'd let go and spin, their skirts catching in the wind like hers once did. She noticed beyond the field of dancers, families stretched out upon rugs, the mothers dotting bread with olives and cheese. No mothers danced, she thought.

She stepped onto the field of dancers, her shoes now hurting her feet badly and her knee bleeding as though wine had spilled down her leg. *If I don't dance, I will be just as the mothers, and I will fall in love and bear children thus.*

Her eyes glazed as the dancers slowed to sing a song she did not recognise. Their voices seemed to glide over the words and they giggled as the chorus hit. They were out there, she thought, every limb free from the desire that ached her so.

"Dancer?" The Baker called from behind her, his eyes still

not believing that the diluted spirit before him could be The Dancer that had been so loved.

"Yes?" she answered, the vestibules of her mind tingling with the anticipation that she was now worthy. Every step she'd taken since she'd left The King, every change she'd made, longed for the proof that this was how she'd become a mother.

"Some salve." He extended his arm and pressed his palm into hers. "For your knee."

The Dancer took the salve, dotting it carefully around the crescent of her knee bleeding crimson. As she sat, tracing the lines of her defeat, she felt the air grow heavy. She caught The Baker's glance and noted that he looked at her like a husband would his bride.

There, she thought. *Fixed.*

✦ THE FACTORY ✦

The Nameless Female stood in line with the other nameless, the one in front standing with his hand outstretched and waiting for the inspector to nod. On days when their callouses burned and the blisters festered, they would be shunted to another department. If fever had set, they'd be sent back to their quarters for the day.

As the line moved to a strict rhythm, The Nameless Female pressed and picked at her blisters. She wanted to make them bleed. Her mind was crushing inward, and this seemed to her like a perfect idea to break the monotony. She plucked at the skin as though it were feathers on a dead duck. She didn't have the words to express the feeling she got from picking—the best she could come up with was congruence, like when you do arithmetic and both sides are equal. The unknown thing inside her seemed understood when the known thing outside of her was painful.

Her eyes had watered this morning as the factory bell had sounded. She knew not what she craved, but that something was off. Her body shook and sweat pooled at her breast. The line moved swiftly until she was standing by an inspector, his booth lined with the same set of protocols like the one she saw yesterday, the officer just as bland.

"Hand!" he rapped in a melancholy demand of procedure.

She offered her hand, fumbling through the pain she'd recently inflicted upon herself. The inspector barely looked before he tagged her wrist with a blue label and pointed to the exit on the left. She knew that exit, and that was not what she wanted. She'd be expected to talk to new nameless, to induct and initiate, to train them for their own impending lifetime of gloom. She muttered under her breath before pointing to the thermometer.

The inspector was aware of the nuisance disrupters could make and chose to quickly comply with her request so he could keep the line moving. He pressed the button upon his desk, a red light piercing the window and landing between her brows.

The light turned green.

"Good." He gestured again to the door on the left. It was specific protocol to not allow disrupters to go back to the lodgings. It was a fact that even the most violent disruptor would, with time, become a productive hand in the factory and a model for a greater society.

She shook her head, frozen and desperate to return to her quarters where her brain could be aired, and she could try to piece together the firing thoughts of her mind. She'd not been able to make sense of them overnight, and then when she slept, it felt she'd been well more active than had she not rested at all. She awoke to the bell exhausted, vivid flashes of faces and places and experiences all settling into her body with a putrid residue.

The inspector quickly pressed the yellow button, and an old mechanical bell rang above his station, sounding much more like a stone hitting a can than the bells she'd heard as a child. He had not the time to question a disruptor, it had not been in his training anyway. This was the protocol, as clearly illustrated upon the sign behind him.

The soldier came and with brutal hands, crushed her shoulders together before lifting her to the door on the left. This, was the consensus, was for her own good. The factory was a saviour, and at times even the mother of a child must discipline her loved ones to keep them safe and on the path to productivity.

Her head was spinning now as the decrepit thoughts swirled within, dizzying her. It was as though the thoughts were leaking from her brain and hitting her gut, her body trying to metabolise them there if the brain could no longer. All she longed for was time to gather each fragment of truth from her cells and wrap them together into one, cohesive story. She didn't know why, but when she left her room, and the bells rang for work, her chest would get heavy. She couldn't breathe. In her room, breath came easy.

She kicked her legs like a wailing child, the soldier mostly unaware as he carried her like a broken doll to the waste bin. Just before he reached the door, The Nameless Female felt a surging flood of bile filling her mouth. Her body grew limp as blood left her limbs and moved to her stomach. The bitter taste made her faint before in one violent heave, she vomited the contents of her torment.

The cleaners swiftly moved in while the soldier pulled at the band on her wrist and replaced it with a black band. She exhaled in a hot, sour collapse of relief. Black means no work, she thought.

The soldier picked her up again by the shoulders, there was no warmth there and nor should she expect it. Affection and its wretched cousin love were the natural enemies to production, invoking a sense of longing and desire. The factory stood to extract the best from everyone, not inject fanciful ideas that lead to heartache and distraction.

He moved her to the side door, at the end of a dark grey wall where the booths would finish. The door opened before him, its sliding automation a sigil of factory glory, albeit but a fading glory as the door rattled and clunked. Crumbling platforms straddled the shuttle tracks. The soldier placed the female in a seat before keying commands into a box on the wall.

The shuttle arrived within seconds, tipping to one side slightly so the platform was met by the step. The soldier pulled the female by the shoulders once more, sitting her on a seat in the empty shuttle. She sat in a seedy fluorescent glow as he walked back through the automatic door and to the inspection room.

The shuttle whirred and squealed its engine to life and left the light of the platform. She rocked from side to side in the darkness, her hands now screaming, searing, as the blood pooled under blisters and dripped to the floor. The shuttle turned dark, bar the light that would flash every few seconds to illuminate the door. She sat alone for several minutes before a voice pierced the silence announcing the next stop.

"S182." The woman's voice was a crucible for The Nameless Female's seething thoughts. Another worker, she thought, as the S-number asserted its position as a workplace. A male one, not much older than her, was pushed by a soldier to a seat further back. She realised the male worker was a true disruptor. She'd merely been considered a disruptor before spewing the contents of her disgusted belly, and then she'd been infirm. This male one was catalogued, a bar value carved into his forehead. The crimson numbers, she thought, were interesting for some reason or another. She stared, trying to understand what made the red so remarkable, her brain so dialled to the linear and fact that it hurt her head to draw a metaphor or stretch to symbolism.

As the shuttle rolled further along, she looked to the male, wondering where the true disrupters were sent. Between the moments where the shuttle went black, she'd have a chance to view the male one's face and try her best to construct a meaning for his being. Each time the light would shine on his face, his eyes glaze over, as though he'd been sedated for the trip. His eyes remained vacant, his lax mouth falling open.

"R373." The voice interrupted her thoughts as the shuttle began to wind down for her stop. She looked across at the male and now noticed he was laughing, gesturing to the sleeping soldier. He darted from his seat over to hers, his smile wide and his lips filled with blood.

"You can't be here," she trembled, equally terrified and awestruck.

"It's okay," he dismissed, "I know this game."

"What about …?" she gestured to the sleeping soldier.

"It's okay, he'll be out for a while. And I'm free until three." The disruptor's mouth turned upward, something she'd not seen too often, and it always made her chest feel lighter when she saw that. But his eyes grew serious, and she wondered what that could mean.

The door opened to the platform. The lights here were a much friendlier hue of gold. The box fluorescents of the factory were replaced by sconces with brass bases, leaning from the wall like delicate stems cradling roses.

"You live here," he observed, nodding his head in questionable approval as he hung himself from the door arch, swaying inward and out. "You're a good girl," he almost mocked, before once again darting back to the seat by the soldier, his grin wild and confident with the bravado of one who was about to win.

She stepped onto the platform before making her way to the lift. She moved upward in the shaking box, the black consuming her except for the dots that would advise the level she was approaching. As the static three dots appeared, and the fourth began blinking, she readied herself to leave the lift and walk the empty hall to her room.

The door buzzed, and she moved from the concrete to the carpet, following the worn trail to the rooms. The light was out by her room, and she tapped at it, wondering what had happened. The light fizzed and sparked, turning on once more before flickering with a pulse. On and off.

She moved into her room, the grey walls closing in as she collapsed onto her bed. Her hands hurt badly now, but her brain was screaming at her to listen even closer. All she wanted to do was forget, but images again flooded her mind. She closed her eyes and, once more, the nightmares erupted.

Bright, striking visions in a cascade devoid of meaning. She'd see the smiling face of the girl she knew as a child and then the male one from the shuttle. She'd see the faces of her parents and a dim recollection of them preparing her for the factory—all of her stories being thrown to the bucket when the armistice was on. Then she would see things she didn't understand: a laughing dog, a lodging by the sea where she stood and sat unproductively, and children running about.

As sweat gripped her skin, she awoke with an obvious fever. Her body was burning. She moved to the bathroom to get some water. As she took a drink, she caught a glimpse of her face in the mirror. The light was abrasive, its awkward placement on one side meant that half of her face was illuminated while the other half was covered by a shadow. Her nose seemed crooked as the light flickered over her head.

She studied her face closer, hoping to see for a moment the eyes of the girl she knew as a child dancing across her forehead. She could hardly be well, she thought to herself, as a smile also sprung atop hers. Golden hair began to grow amongst her own, and dimples soon dotted her cheeks. She was becoming the girl she knew as a child, and while ordinarily, this vision would shake her in terror, something so obviously not real, right now she seemed only mildly curious.

The fever was pulsing through her, and her fragmented brain tended toward following the wild and brilliant cacophony of illusion. Parts of her mind awakened and told her things she'd dare not do before.

"Let's go to the theatre," the voice giggled in delight.

Weary to the bone, she let her feet lead her against the grain of her palpable energy. She had thought herself exhausted, yet now, with this voice maniacally requesting disruption, she found a reservoir within that made walking effortless.

She moved through her door and to the hall, through the elevator and down to the shuttle, where she sat waiting for the next carriage. She knew that she'd send an alert if she were to signal the shuttle and realised after some time sitting on the platform that it could be hours before a shuttle came without her prompt.

She walked from the platform gate and down to the wall, where heavy wire coiled and weaved before sliding down the wall in disrepair. She pulled her foot to the wall and climbed to the top, where she rested her head and felt the breeze upon her skin. Completely unproductive, she lay her for several minutes, mesmerised by this new perspective and tracing the horizon with her eyes.

She sat up before launching herself to the ground, another round of visions assaulted her mind, this time of jumping over fences as a child. She and the girl she knew as a child had often wandered through fields, laughing and dancing, collecting apples and flowers and making rocks look like people. This was when her parents still farmed and before the rain had poisoned the soil.

The rain had killed all of the crops and left the soil sour. The animals too began to take sick and when her father could no longer bear watching their frail bodies rotting, he took a blade to their throats. Her parents all but died that day, their hearts shattered while they beat in despair. They continued to walk and move and smile at their daughter, but their spirits were gone. They trained their daughter to be productive, so the factory could always support her. They took her stories and screamed with fear whenever she played make-believe or danced or sang. Whenever she remembered a fact or followed instruction or read, or counted, they'd smile in approval.

When she finally moved to the factory, the last willing remnants of her youth were stripped. Relationships, the architects had asserted, were most unproductive. They promoted longing and would distract the workers from their duties. Discussions of non-fact would be punished, as the body would behave unpredictably with such. All interaction was to be purely transactional, fact-only, no digressing into story or recollection, which was mostly unproductive yet also led to bodily surges.

Her name, too, was removed.

She walked between buildings, crossing into junkyards and through the crumbling buildings. She found one warehouse that was by far the biggest building she'd ever seen. It was taller than her lodging, with windows so high the light shone right through it. Her footsteps echoed as she immersed herself in the peace, and the magnitude of a building that was now empty. Her gaze melted from one window to the next, the cornices meeting the walls with cracks and furrows. As she walked to the door, a violent picture leapt into sight. Within the gold frame was a standard picture of the factory, the ones that are in every room and cafeteria, but on it was the angry and savage scrawl 'LIES'.

Something completely alien to her body moved within her flesh. She felt her fever rising again, her face sweating as she ran outside for air. Her stomach heaved as she vomited again. She wondered what was wrong, she'd never been sick before, not since the rain first filled the well that was.

She drifted between buildings and over fences before stumbling into the officer's village. She'd discovered it when her hand got stuck in a machine press and she couldn't work in the production sector for weeks. They sent her here to tend to the officers' lodgings and prepare meals. One day her duty was to prepare food for the officers and architects and bring it to the theatre for their evening recreation. She'd never seen a theatre before and found her feet stuck; planted to the ground as a great curtain was painted with moving faces and lights. It was something more than fact, she thought, her entire being not comprehending the sensations in her body.

Now she walked into the foyer, the velvety red carpet the single detail she'd missed when she was first here, absorbing everything that had so captivated her. She remembered the great shining lights that hung from the ceiling, fifty or more bulbs encased in perfect glass prisms that sent light sprawling in every direction. This was where her memory bubbled and questions popped into her mind. Why, mostly, but also what? What did it do, sending all the light in such a way? It seemed unnecessary, unproductive, and possibly wasteful.

But her body registered something she'd not felt since before the rain that killed everything. Her shoulders sunk into their sockets, relaxed, she thought guiltily, as though it was a sin because she was quite clearly standing and relaxed muscles were only for sleep. The bile that had lodged itself in her throat for the past few weeks seemed less bitter too, her breathing softened as she swallowed. Her throat no longer burned.

She moved through to the theatre door, turning the long brass handle. Her blistered hand feeling cool against the metal, she gently pried it open before peeking to see what was inside. Her nose contoured against the door's heavy edge. She saw rows of empty seats, while the screen glowed with the vision of a female and a male. She opened the door a little wider, craning her head to the side to ensure nobody would see her.

"R373." A voice slammed into her ears and rattled away before her eyes adjusted to the dim lighting so she could make out who'd shouted at her. She'd never before been identified by a sentry as her tower prefix. She assumed they would check her wrist for her identity code, but then again, she'd never ventured from where she was supposed to be before.

She turned, but it wasn't a guard. The Nameless Female

gasped in shock. The male one from the shuttle now stood in full light before her. His smile barely fitting upon his face as his eyes were wide and fizzing with something she recognised as mania.

"What are you doing here?" He laughed, knowing that disrupters were known to pop up anywhere and not be tethered to the rules of the factory. This young lady thought, he thought, this was fascinating. She was an R tenant, she lived in the best workers tower and must have been a walking citadel, only those with perfect recall of facts made it to the R towers.

She moved past him, thinking if she pretended she was meant to be here, he would not know the difference. She sat at a seat, before arching her neck to the large curtain with the moving picture. A male, dressed in a black suit with a bow on his neck, held the hand of a female who was wearing a robe that matched the sky, yet it had no buttons, sat tight across her chest and waist, and fell to her feet. A vision flashed before her of her mother wearing something like that once, long before the rain fell when The Nameless Female was still very much a baby.

They moved, arms outstretched to one another before her body would spin inward to his, and he would hold her against his body. She looked up to him, and he pressed his mouth to her head. And then, it happened again, and again, the film on loop.

The Nameless Female was mesmerised. He was a prince, she thought, remembering the stories from her childhood, and she was a princess. She watched the same cycling vision over and again before the male from the shuttle laughed at her and broke her focus.

"You know it's broken, right?" He knew she'd never watched a full film before, her fascination with this simple sigil overcoming her with something he'd call feelings and she'd call non-fact.

"Yes," she lied, her face steaming and her gut churning. She stood up, walked down the aisle, and pushed her way through the 'Staff Only' door.

An aging janitor tended with devotion to the canisters that lay before him. He looked up for a moment, as though he'd heard something and been disturbed, but after looking directly at The Nameless Female, his glance returned to his work and mending the broken reels. Workers rarely had the capacity to question their surroundings. Their tasks being so programmed into them that outlying possibilities never sparked within their brains. They'd been trained to look only to the task at hand—disrupters would have little effect on their productivity.

The male from the shuttle moved past her now and inspected the projector with the same maniacal smile he'd shown in the shuttle. He pulled a silver tool from his pocket, and started to screw and unscrew parts and dials, before taking the spool and carving out a long, meandering line through the film, and then returning to his seat.

He sat, again with his mouth upturned but this time his eyes widened and his whole body looked softer. He looked at her, his mouth flashing more teeth than she recalled seeing, nodding his head as he called for her to sit.

The female followed him back into the theatre, thinking he must have repaired that which he said was broken. As she sat down though, the putrid remnants of unsynced visual and muzak, the prince walking a lonely shadow with his nose collapsing under a syphilitic sky. The princess ran from him, her corset unbound and ruffles askew, scars on her wrists and track-marked arms.

He sat watching her, knowing her disconnect would be echoed through the soldiers that were programmed to attend this evening. The soldiers believed themselves privy to all knowledge, but their movies only showed what was approved by the state. He took great pride in the changes he'd make to their movies, improvements, he believed. No more golden premises of love and delight, spurring the soldiers to procreate with their compliant wives. He'd haunt them, shock them until they sufficiently questioned the rules they'd been following. He could spend years liberating one worker at a time, or one movie disrupting the entire class of soldiers.

He watched her face twitch as her eyes adjusted to this new scene. Her lips pursed and her hands clenched, her breathing became audible against the scratch of Muzak.

"What?" The Nameless Female asked, her words searing.

"What what?" His smile now dialled to full exposure as his eyes narrowed to watch her gasp, her body drawing whatever it could to make sense.

"What happened to the pictures?"

"What pictures?" Again his grin widened, and his body relaxed.

"The people!" Her breathing became louder, the inhale slightly less than the exhale.

"They're there." His voice was again cool and not pressed at all by her nerve.

"They're not." It almost fell a whimper this time, yet still, his smile broadened.

"How are they not?"

"Because they're not." Her arms flailed, pointing toward the screen as though he'd simply missed seeing it like he'd know if he looked.

"Tell me the facts." His smile calmed and he settled in his seat to listen.

She pointed to the screen. "Before her mouth was up. Now it's down."

"But that's just angles," he said, mining her for further clarity.

"But it's more."

"More than what?" he prodded. "Facts?"

Her nostrils flared. She thought he must know what she was saying, but his words, his questions, seemed that he was clueless. She looked again at the picture, and for a moment the princess looked healthy, dancing in a garden, her hair in a loose braid and a white hat tied around her chin. This settled The Nameless Female, her eyes beaming at the screen.

"What is it?" he asked, as her lips peeled open and the corners moved upward. She nodded, as though in agreeance but not sure what.

The Muzak whirred as though the reel had been turned in the wrong direction, or the tape had become stuck on its wheel. The princess's dress began to rip from the bottom upward, the sleeves being pulled from the cuff and her bloodied arms once more spread across the screen.

The Nameless Female breathed in, a deep, accusatory inhale as she stared at him with eyebrows coursing deeper into her sockets. "What did you do?"

"She's still there." He smiled, but this time he seemed almost scared of her reaction. There was a wild there that wasn't before.

"She's not!" Her voice screeched as she half-stood over him.

"Tell me the facts," he said, his words anchoring her back to her training.

"She's different. Her face. Her arms. Her dress …"

"But what does it matter?"

"Because before I could breathe, and now I can't."

"But why?"

"Why what?

"Why can't you breathe?"

"Because my body changed."

"Why?"

Her mouth stitched shut and her breath became charged with the same desperation she'd felt in the factory earlier that morning. She sat, unable to answer what the changing picture meant. There were facts, the angle of the mouth and the bloodied arms, but this was something inside of her. Maybe a parasite, she thought, moving within her, causing her pain.

"It's fury," the male from the shuttle said, laughing as he shared with her a conceptual diamond.

"What's fury?"

"In your body, that's fury. You're furious that I changed the picture. You're furious that you go to the factory, you're furious that you have no beauty."

Her head fell to one side as she scanned the disrupter for facts. There was, indeed, something in her body that weaved and changed, lending her to sickness that was seemingly growing by the day.

"You live in fury," he said, this time the smile wiped from his face and his eyes locked to hers. He pointed to her hand, where she'd tugged at the blisters so much her whole palms had swelled and festered.

"What's fury?" she asked again.

"It's a non-fact … but it's real."

Bile returned to her mouth, her head had swallowed his words neatly, before setting them to burrow into her mind like little rats hunting for crumbs. The dichotomy, swimming through her brain and meeting opposition in every fact that she knew, facts were the only 'real', there were facts, and then production, which were facts in action. These were the only things.

And yet, she was standing here, in a place that defeated reason. She understood her capacity for facts were obviously not as great as the officers and architects. They must know

something more than her that deemed such splendour
necessary.

"Don't you ever wonder why it rained?" the disruptor
asked, plucking something from her being that he saw sitting
dormant.

"It rained because the clouds were filled with evaporated
poison."

"But why?"

"Because there was an accident, and it had spilled into the
river."

"How?"

"Human error."

"Which human?"

She noticed her body starting to get hot again, as sweat
stung her hands. She needed to sit with the blood flooding
from her head to feet.

"A stupid one … like you," she said, glaring at the numbers
plastered to his head. He was a disruptor, he obviously knew
nothing. But something picked away at her logic, mainly
because this place that she stood in, while she succumbed to
the understanding that she was not smart enough to know the
facts for its existence, something else had risen in her body
while she'd been here. The lights in the foyer had made her
shoulders move down, as though she was preparing for sleep.
And the pictures of the dancing prince and princess, her chest
felt different. It was a non-fact, but a real reaction.

She stared at his face, harshly inspecting the combination
of gestures it held. He didn't dismiss her, and yet something

in his face was saying he didn't agree. He was nodding, not with her, but at her.

"What?" she demanded, the blood now rising to her head and priming her tongue for exchange.

"Feelings."

"What?"

"Feelings," he repeated, slowly and considerately.

"What? Like when you cut yourself and it hurts?"

"Exactly. Except you don't cut yourself".

"How could it hurt if you don't cut yourself?" His mania now fuelled her rising voice.

"That's feelings—a non-fact, but real." He watched her start to shift from one foot to the other, his emotional radar sounding. "Like now, you feel confused, and a bit furious."

Her body did feel something, but it was nausea and the prickles lining her throat that caused her discomfort. "I feel sick," she said, searching for an air vent, or an exit, or somewhere to fall to the floor. She leaned onto the chair, propping herself with her beaten hand.

"Where does that come from?" He pulled her further into her body.

"My stomach."

"Before that."

"My nerves."

"And why that?"

"Because they're being excited."

"By what?"

She sat now and wrapped her hands around her head as

they pooled into her legs. She felt awful, and his questions were making it worse.

"By your stupid questions!" she shouted.

"How?" He was amused now, knowing what he was alluding to was precisely what she was experiencing.

"STOP!! You're making me feel … SOMETHING!"

"Feelings," he said, walking back to the projector room. "Non-fact, but real."

✦ THE BIG WILD ✦

It's wilder there, where pegasus roam with the peacock. The Dreamer's eyelids parted just a moment, enough for her to see the white walls peeling flecks of paint in her bedroom, before she closed them again, willing the vision's return.

There'd been a time when science both piqued and quenched her curiosity. She'd look to the world with wonder, awe smacking her cheeks with the realisation that things could be proven. But now, as she'd rise for work and sit at the microscope, watching enzymes and microbes dance and disappear, it all seemed much the same. Every day, the same. Every experiment, the same. All melting reason into the same crucible, bending science to accommodate mystery.

The sun beat through the window upon her closed eyelids, capillaries lacing like gossamer calling her to rouse. She sat up, eyes tempting to once again shut before she sunk her feet to the floor. Carpet brushed upon her bare toes, as she walked from her room into the kitchen, flicking the jug to boil.

Her eyes fell upon photographs of her childhood, her with a horse, her with her grandmother, and she'd realised that behind her eyes those memories never looked that way. The pictures seemed to lie, just like her family would when they'd talk about the past. They'd recall dully, as though they'd forgotten the thrill. It was as though they'd lived another time, another place, one without her.

As a child, wild was expected. She'd run for hours through the forest, her face beaming with the enraptured glory of freedom. Her toes would be muddied, scratches from the brambles etching a delicate symphony across her milky skin. The air was crisp and pure and laced with the grace of God. She'd run, and hide, and climb the firs and build little castles upon the branches.

She remembered vividly, standing under pine as mystical beings would gulp their first breath, and giddily squeal themselves into form. She would think it, and then they would be there. Sprites would flutter past her eyes, with a luminance not bound by the earthly laws of vision.

She never questioned the magic. She never thought with the cells in her brain to oppose the blossoming thoughts and sparks of bliss.

The curious day came when she found herself standing naked, like an Asclepius rising from the luscious earth, vines snaking their tender shoots around innocent limbs. An adult appeared, in quite an adult way, saying it was time to tend to the garden. His hands gripped a piece of machinery that growled as he switched it on. She watched as he swung it from his hip, branches and grasses falling to the ground.

She'd not yet grasped the concept of deception but would one day come to understand that sometimes adults, doing adult things, would not tend to be as wondrous as she'd wished. As trees fell upon the forest floor, her tiny sprites burst. One followed by another, they'd go from gold to dust, from shimmering to shadow. When she searched for them, she instead found pretty little rows of flowers, tethered to frames.

How quaint, she thought. Her fingers tracing the lines of petals upon hardwood trellis. She heard a rhythmic crash of hammers overhead and watched workmen pounding nails. A white frame arched to the blue, roses blooming beneath.

Her awe stretched beyond the comforts she'd understood of family; that people could make things, real things, big things, and that there was more to the world than wild. Man could make things to capture dreams and the dreams of flowers and house them and keep them safe.

Every day, the men would return, each improvement further invoking delight. Walls to keep her warm from the wild and biting wind, a floor to keep her toes tidy, and curtains to shield from the sun. And then, came the roof, and her last free breath.

At night she would look up, her eyes searching for the prism of stars she'd felt held in, the one she believed to be home. She knew not of star people, but in that sky, she felt a womb. She'd shut her eyes and see her darling sprites, see the trees as they'd dance with her, she'd see the music wind through the valley.

Eventually, the visions would melt into sleep, where she'd believe them to be just a dream, just imagination. Amnesia filled the void where magic once swam.

"Haven't you heard?" A worker one day poked at her arm while she was walking to school. "Earth was a seed that grew over billions of years, not seven days. There is no God."

"Oh," she said, as she wondered how long 'billions of years' was. A lot, she thought. So much that she couldn't possibly argue with a number bigger than anything she'd ever counted. It had to be true.

The dreams bled dry soon after that. Within the crevices that ached for wild, she'd deposit more and more scientific facts. Reason would somehow conquer her cravings. It was real, tangible, replicable. An equation of probabilities.

The kettle clicked and steam shot from the spout, warm on her face. She was sure it used to whistle. She slowly tipped the boiling water over coffee so that a crema would appear as though it was far from the espresso she'd had in Florence. Oh Firenze, her heart pounded at that memory. It felt so brilliant, a kaleidoscopic journey through sight and sensation. Things seemed more alive.

She walked to the couch, hoping to catch the last of the morning sun beaming through the window before it swung to the north and left her window. Her house would be dark again then, the grey would descend, and her room would be cold.

As she readied herself to sit, a crack in the window caught her eye. It was deep and cleft it's way from the top corner and almost all the way to the bottom. While the window was old, the fissure appeared to be not of age, but something much more symbolic, like a river coursing over rocks, inviting her to slide in and feel it rush over her body.

She moved close to the window, her face cocked to one side as though understanding would reach her more fully there. Her eyes followed the lines from top to bottom, and then upward again. It smelled of old wood and aging glass—a familiar smell—but through the crack drifted summer, the smell of jasmine and party and play.

When she moved back and shifted her head to the other side, brilliant and luminous colour struck her, as though a whip was calling her attention. She'd not seen a rainbow in many years. Her lips rounded as though she was about to whistle but just the slightest of breaths slipped through.

Through there, she thought, was wild. It called her, louder, drawing her heart as though it pulled from her spine. She knew in moments, this would all be gone; the sun would pass above her rooftop, her living room once more suspended in grey.

Her heart fled from her, racing ahead, pulsing blood through her arms and forcing her fingers to pry the crack. She peeled at the glass, as though she would peel at curtains, hands stretching the space within as the window opened from its ripped centre.

Light flooded her, all seven colours of the rainbow, and their offspring, bled into her body. Her arms fell limp by her side as her eyes and mouth widened beyond the face that kept them. Her heart stopped now, as though it too stood in awe.

"Don't go there", she heard them say. "There are vengeful gods and nothing is certain."

Had she not been captured in the light of wild, she may have listened. Like when she said she wanted to move to Florence and grow her own food. This time, she stood still in the flood of bliss, and their words wouldn't easily shake her. She chewed each word, looking for substance, looking for something that could sit in her cells and offer her nourishment, but here she heard only their fear.

Beyond their words, again she felt a thread drawing her, from her spine and through her heart. This time she yielded to it, allowing it to pull her body—her legs and feet—up to stand within the recess. Here, she realised, was the schism of science and myth, if the light carried her across, she could never return.

She tried to recall what was on the other side. The last time she'd seen it was permafrost over fields. She felt willed and forced at once. As she stepped down she felt ice melting under her warm feet. Her nightgown billowed and caught against broken glass, catching and fraying.

Amongst her instincts, she found herself stepping timidly. Every step was careful, each nerve in her foot shying from the ice beneath. The rainbow now danced exquisitely. It had moved from the window and swirled around her in a vortex of radiant colour.

I could slide, she thought, her inner voice an octave higher than that she'd normally use. A smile erupted on her face, wild, like when she was young.

She pushed one foot forward, the other following. It was slow but it felt new. She'd not felt new in years. She continued until her breath grew strong, and she found herself upright, breathing crisp air and legs sliding freely. She felt a stricture snap, as though she'd stretched the leash so taut that it severed. Science and fact seemed not to matter so much anymore.

She skated wildly. On and on and on, her legs reaching further and further, until she was quite sure her hips would be pulled from their sockets. Her heart pounded with excitement, with the feeling she'd recalled from her past as purpose. Snow fell upon her, melting as it touched sanguine limbs.

The fields opened to a great expanse, perhaps a lake, she thought, when it wasn't winter. The clouds sat black overhead, not at all pleasant and yet she felt a warmth touching her, as though those clouds had once birthed and fed her.

The thread that had pulled her now shone golden like a tap had been turned and creation pulsed through it. She felt her back, like a socket, lighting up as the rope pulled through her heart and off to the distance. She saw it passing through splintered wood, a fence, and then beyond the brilliant glow of wild.

That's where God lives, she thought.

And then she heard the singing. The tiny voice, a child in rapturous delight unaware of listening ears. The sun beamed down upon the paddock over the fence, an abrupt line of ominous cloud and the ice that stung at her face now yielding to the immense beauty of golden rays flooding from above, touching the skin of a darling faery as she sang in ethereal timbre.

Through a broken nook in the fence, she could see her

brushing a fern frond over a pond, The Dreamer's eyes adjusting to the incoming brilliance of colour, as she peered upon wings aglow in swirling illumination. The delicate voice rising and falling, the hue following her song as if dancing.

This world, she knew, was not real. All of the facts had told her so. Fae did not exist and the spectrum available to our human eyes would remain as it was. The vivid and striking combination of colour and tone and depth and luminosity was all but an illusion, her mind deceiving her.

Besides, there were vengeful gods.

To enter this world would be a sin, an insult and a betrayal of all that humans had realised through science. There would be no shelter from the rain. And the howling of the wolves would keep her awake at night. But it felt real. She felt herself a magnet to the garden in which she sat, that winged beauty.

Her feet now tingled, every fibre of her skin alert to the underbrush by the fence. Pine needles poked at her ankles. It didn't hurt or sting like she remembered they could, it felt more like a greeting, like they were saying 'Hello. I'm here.'

She wondered if this was how connection felt. She'd thought she had connections back there, back in the real world, but now it all seemed dull. The lady at the grocers, the professor at the lab, even the friend she travelled with. It all seemed so safe, all a transaction in an attempt to own something greater.

This was rich, each of her senses pinged with impending bliss. Her tongue sparked as she tasted the air. Her ears felt heavy as though they filled with syrup, listening to the fairy sing. Her eyes misted and rippled, like a pebble in a pond. Everything appeared with greater brilliance, colours seemed to both contrast and merge, like they were so bright they bled into one another.

She pulled at a fence paling, her mind thinking that a garden this decadent must surely be fortified. She'd never get in, she thought, God lives there. She'd almost surrendered to her thought when her finger flicked itself at the fence, sending the paling high into the sky.

Another thought, this one from somewhere within the thread, scraped itself up her spine as though etching a law in her psyche. *This world has no law. The more I am connected, the more it yields to my will.*

She found herself inside the wall. She didn't recall stepping or squeezing herself between the palings and yet she stood well past the fence and not far from the fairy. She allowed the vines to wrap their tendrils around her legs and creep ever slowly up her tender body. She succumbed to the entwinement. It was glorious, she thought, rapturous.

The fairy, now fully aware of her presence, moved with her fern frond, brushing it so softly over the pond that the leaves left an imprint. The frond brushed over rock, and then swept across her toes, before coming to rest on her bicep, as one would their hand upon a friend.

"You're back," said the fairy. Her singing voice sounded nothing at all like her spoken voice, which was almost shrill, and as though her vocal cords sounded every letter as its own, separate entity.

The Dreamer's legs began to itch as the vines gripped her tighter. She'd not been here before, she thought, although it did not feel completely unfamiliar. She felt bound now, her legs squirming to be free.

"Think it," said the fairy, gesturing to the vines.

The fairy's words settled upon her, much like the clouds before, with a sense of nourishment, as though they were connected beyond anything cognitive. She thought of her legs before, when the pine needles had tapped at her ankles. She'd not even finished her thought when the vines unfurled from her legs and stroked at her feet.

The frond, which had been at her arm, now rested beside the fairy. The warmth of her welcome now settled to ease. The fairy turned, the tip of her toes balancing her entire body like a ballerina as she walked back to the pond. There was an aching familiarity, thought The Dreamer, although she couldn't recall the details. It seemed something like this would cleave itself to memory; the colours, the scent of moss upon rocks and damp earth, and the taste of life on her tongue. She couldn't remember any of it, yet nothing surprised her.

She followed tiny toe prints sunken in mud to the rock by the pond. Every step settling her into a groove she knew to be more wondrous, more real than anything she'd felt back in the real world. Glee spilled from her heart, pouring to the earth, anchoring her there. She sat on the rock, it was hard not unlike the rocks back home, but this one seemed to cradle her like a mother would a baby.

"You dream?" The fairy asked. Again, just two words.

The Dreamer was struck by the simplicity of her conversation and its capacity to carry so much. She'd been accustomed to elaborate conversation, longer, more words, more context to describe the longing that indescribable.

"Sometimes," said The Dreamer, however, halfway through she realised the question was not what she thought. The fairy scrunched her nose as a child might when an adult tried to trick.

The faery went back to singing, each note rippling and waving and seeping into The Dreamer's cells as if tuning an instrument or casting a message into stone. Her mind tried to wander, again to this being myth but her body disagreed. Her shoulders settled into their cuffs, no longer drawn to her ears with tense and toughened muscle. Her breath danced in respiration, inspiration, expiration, a circular effortless embrace as her heart slowed to the percussive rap of the faery song. Each foot and every nerve spindle responding to the tantalising texture of earth underfoot. She could smell ripe plums and jasmine blossoms carried from the hedge by the wall.

Something swelled within her, amongst the sensual harvest she feasted on, was a deep resonance that this was home. That this, in all its exquisite intricacies, was real and right.

Had she been any further immersed in the wonder, she'd probably not heard the bell. The sharp twinkle of a laboratory timer reminding her that cultures bloomed back there, that petri dishes awaited.

She took a single step toward the thicket lining the fence,

before turning back to her fairy friend. Wrapping hands within hands, she felt blood pulsing under skin, but hardly knew whose veins they coursed. There, in that very moment, she felt the great nexus of mundane and magic rendering together.

She drew a breath and pushed her body through the hedge. There were no palings this time, jasmine had grown thick in its place but the limbs and branches opened as she willed her way through. She looked to the field, expecting the lake and ice, yet a ravine appeared in its stead. A rope bridge strung from cliff face to cliff face, the smell of fresh-cut oak settled upon her nose.

As she walked across, she felt her body tightening, as though preparing for the finite world awaiting her. Her shoulders rose in their cuffs until they sat somewhere near her ears. Her mind, cast itself beyond the bridge, beyond the whistling abyss below, and to the real world and her work.

When she arrived on the other side of the cliff, she saw the door to her laboratory. The fluorescent light flooded through the tiny window. Here, she realised, it felt even more an assault than it did while she worked. The colours burst with saturation beyond mere sight, flushing the body and emulsifying within. The fluorescence would stop at her face, hanging there, as though it would never belong in her heart.

She opened the door to the lab, her colleagues not at all disturbed by the intrusion. They'd been collating data, swiping litmus beside a reference, and typing results. She knew they'd been working with sulphur, yet she couldn't smell a thing. The walls, their coats, the lights and tables, all seemed a variant of the same shade of beige.

The Dreamer walked to her microscope, grabbing a slide from the drawer. She took a pen from a cup and belt it upon the glass slide, cracking a long fissure from the top corner to near the base. She clasped her fingers around it, holding it up to the humming fluorescent light.

She'd not known exactly what would happen, only that she was drawn by the same thread that drew her to the fairy. At worst, she thought, it would be an act of destruction. But what beamed through the tiny sliver seemed beyond anything she'd known. The same light that had burst through her broken window now shot through that cracked slide. Through it, however, was not the same icy field that she skated while wind bit at her cheeks. As she moved the slide around the room, she saw science through the lens of a miracle.

There was something wild there. Big. And wild.

WHEN THE WIZARD DIES

He called himself The Wizard, but he was really just a sailor. He stood like an ox, several feet tall and towering over the men and boys that joined him on his ship. In certain light, it would seem that his head hovered somewhere near the top of the masthead. His hands, beefy and furious, calloused with the salty mix of sea and rope.

His voice was gnarled and cracked with the carcass of a northern accent. There was nothing fleshy, nothing soft, no juice or meat. Words stripped to their bone without the balm of concern.

His feet would pound heavy across the aging decks. Aging, indeed, but The Wizard would have them scrubbed and polished every day with the same dutiful reverence he'd had when he first bought his Magdalena. It wasn't the custom for sailors to own their own ships; ordinarily, they'd wait at the ports or be employed by a boat master to sail for trade, or sometimes petty wars that were easily won. But he'd never drunk the ale or paid for women and instead, he'd managed to save a decent amount of coin.

He'd not set about to buy his own boat, yet as his money grew he thought it the only thing he could possibly be happy to spend it on. Sailing, the ocean, navigation defined him more than anything else ever could. When he was docked a melancholy would grip him, his words would become clipped and he'd yell to the crew to hasten their trips to port. His teeth would clench so hard that occasionally one would pop from his mouth, a yellowed and chipped glint of his wrath, spat to the water.

While he waited at the port, he'd hear the meows of cats, each coming to him for food. He suffered humans not, but for the cats, his stance would relax, his voice softened to almost a song, and he'd hand them the scraps that his crew refused to eat. It infuriated him mostly, that they would pick and choose their fill as though food had a hierarchy.

He made his crew return at night, knowing that if he let them spend the night in the town they'd be sick with ale and reek of women, their clumsy hands working slower than usual. His shouts and insults barely reaching their pea brains as they'd set the mast and loading the last of the cargo.

His was the only boat leaving this day, there was a storm to come and it was said to scream in fury. The Wizard revelled in this though; he'd sit at the bow, inhaling the oncoming winds and tracing the tapestry of pink cloud with his eyes. He couldn't bear to be at port, that was as good as death to him. He couldn't bear to sit idle and wait. A storm, a monster storm, would separate sailor from sissy. He'd seen men that regaled in glory from fights in the tavern, real men, they would call themselves, huddled under crates whimpering like kittens abandoned by their mothers.

As his men heaved at the anchor, his eyes directed to the shank before his mouth matched the dripping arms, wide to his ears, upturned in a primal excitement. Resentment and impatience now folded to the electric, thrumming hiss of winds impregnated with the thrill of complete and utter submission. He'd ride the liminal now, as the waves and sky would crash into one, each man aboard at the mercy of the Gods they did or didn't serve.

He'd made himself a myth, The Wizard. His dying father had brought him to a dock when he was barely even a boy. Young legs stretched like snakes to his wiry frame, ribs popping through skin so white his gut would pulse pink beneath it. This sick old man who had found his mother broken as a child and married her and broke her some more. He'd beat them both until their mouths were so busted they'd not hunger for food. His mother, so destroyed by her own tormented fate that she'd not reach for her son, not hold nor comfort him, not stroke his hair that was matted with blood.

"He's too small," the boatmaster had said that day, dismissing the old man with barely a glance.

"He won't eat much," the father batted back.

"Or sir, he'll eat more than the men twice his size."

"He will scrub, and polish. He is good at that. Don't need no strength for that, just discipline."

"And something tells me he has had ample of that." The boatmaster's eyes landed on a scar that coursed from under the child's arm, down his side and across his belly.

"He knows his place," the father trumpeted proudly.

"I'm sorry, sir, this boat is full."

His father shuffled in now what appeared to be desperation. Both he and his wife had taken ill and his father needed the boy to bring him coin. Even one month at sea would pay back what sat in his pocket now.

"I have coin," the father said, pawing for his pouch.

The boatmaster shook his head at the old man. Ale seeped from the withered skin with a stench greater than even his worst deckhands. He mostly thought of other humans as little more than stock, but the boy had met his eyes with a sturdy mix of staunch determination and broken innocence that he shuffled the beds in his head.

"How much?"

"Fifteen coi—eleven, eleven coins. It's not much but it's all I have and he will work hard." The father's manner lightened as optimism returned.

"Will you work hard?" The boatmaster now addressed the boy directly, the father's pride assaulted as the boatmaster met the boy's eyes with respect.

"Of course he will," the father said, his head barely reaching his son's shoulders.

"Is the boy mute?" the boatmaster asked, knowing this pathetic ego would not be silenced unless offended.

"No," the son spoke firmly, "and yes, I will work harder than any of the men you have here, and for longer."

The boatmaster scoffed at this. "Do you know I have men twice your size that have worked for many years?"

"I'm sure they have, sir," replied the boy, "but I bet they all want to go home, too."

The father, somewhat dull and unaccustomed to rhetoric took his time to understand what his son was saying. He had barely scraped the edges of his understanding when the boatmaster reached out his hand.

"Fifteen coins. He will sleep on the deck." He pushed the boy onto the boat, grabbing the old man's money while his tongue singed his lips. He'd met many a handful of scoundrel in his life, but that man set his blood ablaze like no other.

True to his word, the boy spent his days with his hands in muddied water, claws snared around the brush like an eagle with the bloody heart of its prey. The brush, he thought, was the only way out of his pitiful little life back in the village. If he did this right, he could kill the little boy that his father had tossed around the house like the core of an apple he'd eaten in rage.

The boy looked about one supper at the men and their drink, barely eating their bread as they swallowed the wine, mouths gaping wide and willing. One man, who had barely touched a crumb and rested his elbow to the table, propped his hand as it rocked with the cup. He sang and shouted as though in great celebration or ceremony. *He prefers to drink the wine than eat*, thought the boy.

With tiny hands, he reached towards the man's plate. Each of his fingers was purple with peeling skin—the soft skin of a babe erupting with the brutality of manhood. As he neared the jewels of bread, the man stood slightly and threw his arm and struck the boy's cheek, a boulder of bone and tendon slamming against the scars left by a murderous father.

The boy, silenced but not sorrowed, walked to the stairs and up to the deck. If he could kill that boy, he thought, he could craft another. He could make himself whomever he chose to be. He needed to kill that boy or the remnants that his father had wrapped in a bundle and deposited on the ship. He thought to the gods and the heroes and men that he'd seen by the port as a child when he'd follow his father's finger to pilfer their careless belongings. He'd been quite the gifted thief, as a child at least, but as he grew closer to manhood, his frame became longer, his limbs less graceful. He'd clunk and sway his way under tables and about the market, each movement a great gesture as his arms stretched wide from his body. This was about the time his father sought to excise him from his 'care'.

He was pathetic, he knew this. But, as was the gift of many a drunkard's spawn, he had witnessed the faces of a changeling father. How one could go from completely wretched and furious, to tender and melodic, singing and swaying in bliss. Then, when the drink would consume him more than he consumed it, he'd slide his burgundy tongue to the side of his mouth and bite, and violence would fill him. Each face embodied in fullness. Each word struck with the temporal grasp of identity.

If it's so, and one may simply choose their face, their skin, the legend of their story, then why should he not embrace his own ideals of who is great and what he shall be. The next night at supper, he sat with his wine in hand and stared at the man who had last night struck him. He rolled the glass, around and around, the wine swishing and swirling much the same as the thoughts that would roll through his head. His eyes, locked to the man, watching him slosh and shout and finish his own wine before he realised the boy was staring.

The boy, with a slight and wry smile carved on his face, looked down to the full cup and then back to the man. He pushed the cup in the smallest gesture a few thumb-widths toward the man. The man at once leant over to grab the prized nectar, but the boy pulled his cup back.

"No," he said, pointing to the man's plate.

And that was how his legend grew. He never takes to drink. He eats the meat of two.

Over time, the meat would seep into his skin, settle and ripen. His pallid and bony arms grew full and bronze. Curves filled his body as muscles pulled tautly and bulged with the heaving of rope and rum. He'd learn to lift barrels alone with barely a strain, as lesser men would stumble aboard two abreast.

When his mother died, he stopped sending money home. His father could rot. The boy would finally be dead and the legend could live in his limbs.

The Wizard stood at the bow, as was his custom, whenever they left port. His face beat with the burning primal rays of sun, cutting through the glassy water and slicing into his eyes. He'd often woo the dawn, talking to her like the other men would speak to the women in the bawdies, inhaling her and holding her scent within, lingering before the exhale. Oh, how he loved her so. He'd watch as birds basked in peach glow threading their way across the sky, seemingly celestial before they'd squawk and land on the port all ravenous and feral.

His hair, now reaching well beneath his shoulders in an icy glaze of white and crimson, floated and fell as the ship floated and fell, slicing through the waves. He stood there, smothered in glory, chest pounding to the sky as each heartbeat thumped and boomed and his arms swung limp like a barometer, tuning himself to the dawn and her wisdom.

He took command once more when the bay expanded into a vast surge, and the men watched the final glint of the port with sorrow, or joy, or anger. His voice rumbled over the decks as he set his men to work, the sound that would rupture the sky as he belted each word from his fleshy tongue.

On this day, the commands were brief. "Due west," he called as they set course to move silk and spices. There was extra coin invested in this trip, as the boat was bound to roll wildly about the waves. Summer was notoriously the time when storms would swell and gape, lightning slicing the sky. When the gods awakened from the ample spring celebrations, ambrosia soured in their veins.

The Wizard revelled in the challenge. His muscles primed with the vigour of horses, staunch in purpose and striding ever forward. His face glowed and his belly roared with laughter.

He'd been waiting, as the dawn had whispered her wisdom

to him alone. Around noon, she'd said. An hour or so had passed since the sun sat in his highest, holiest throne above. The vapours of distant petrichor would sweep his nose and flood him with memories of those first trips he'd made as a boy, the dusty and rocky islands soaking the rain into their veins as it fell. His nose now attuned to the familiar scent, he'd sense its strength, the direction, the soil upon which it fell and chart his course in response.

That was why they, too, called him The Wizard. He'd conjure men by might and magic. The clouds, the stars—they became his tools. He'd manipulate the forces and steer the boat or steer the stars, whichever seemed the greatest feat. He'd reach his hand to the night sky, heavy fingers scraping the curtain of black as the ship would sternly shift its gaze to a new course. He'd sleep still upon the deck, each nerve saturated in the air of the sea, a complex set of spindles each tingling and fizzing with every detail.

The faint but steady drops now staining the deck, their lazy pattern spilling onto the wood and melting before drying under the searing and anxious sun. He sensed a god had come to visit, the pull of the boat as wind filled the sail, the slapping of waves against the hull. He sought the cook to prepare supper early, they'd not long had tea, but his bones simmered with anticipation of what was to come.

With supper, a silence befell. The air was pregnant beyond the light mist that fell. Even the rowdiest of his men, the southerners, held their tongue in awe. If they had not the sense or awareness of The Wizard, him calling an early supper had sufficiently tightened their suspicions. The men that had been in his tenure for a great number of years knew he was burrowed in a strict routine.

As they sat in the mess, the only sounds were the occasional clank of iron cups to the table, and bread being dropped back to plates. The scraping of forks would see these Neanderthal eaters suddenly apologetic and demure. The mist turning to drops, and then a soporific roar. The boat swayed and groaned as the wind picked up, a cradle on the sea.

The men held down their plates as those with a hefty appetite managed to finish their dishes. They gathered their utensils and piled them into the sink before the night turned white under a crack of lightning that lingered for minutes. They scrambled upstairs, one man sliding from the step as the boat arched its back to the sky and slammed the hull against its rugged bed. His brow gushing crimson and coursing to his lips where it pooled with the sticky nervous sweat that had stuck to his stubble.

The Wizard now hollered and laughed at the sky. The gods were here, he knew it. Through a slither of broken cloud, he could see the stars stretched in a line over the horizon. A formation for war, or glory, or battle and change. They hung, watching him curiously as they readied themselves for the show, the grandest entertainment, a mortal wizard and the wrath of the tempest.

The boat now rocked and arched its way from side to side, waves crashing and revolting in all directions. Thunder boomed above and the sky sang in its melody, light flooded the black night as it would crack and whip and bolt in fury.

The men now hung on where they could. The timid remnants of boy and men being strewn from stern to bow as the boat lurched and swelled, the rain now pounding like fire upon their skin.

"Below deck!" The Wizard belted, a smile wide beyond his ears. He'd watched from the masthead as his men scuttled like vermin before the catcher. He pulled at the sailcloth, folding it in its rope so that, come morning, he could unfurl it untorn.

This was something exceptional, he thought as the wind softened against his face. The boat yielded to a slow, gentle rise and the rain settled back to mist. He held the mast, foot upon peg, as he breathed the wild air. His laugh boomed through the sky, as he, The Wizard, readied himself for a second assault. This was living, he thought, really living. Not ale, not women, not coin or land. He locked his legs to the mast, reaching his arms with a span that would carry most men twice, drawing the horizon together with thick hands, pulsing, throbbing, shaking as he lifted the cloud.

He'd not had an intention, more of a compulsion. As he lifted higher and his arms crushed together, rain squeezed like pomegranates, dripping thick and syrupy. The ball of black cloud now pulsed and moaned between his fingers, as he leaned it back over his shoulder, sinew and scar glistening, he hurled it to the horizon like a rock. It squealed through the air like a meteor, screaming with rage as its shrieking passage thundered the sky. In a final and daunting *boom*, the ball crashed to the sea.

The atmosphere, at that moment, vanished. The air was still, there was no cawing from birds, no waves breaking. Night had swallowed the sky, and the stars stretched themselves across the heavens like a goddess in her bed. This vacuous and delicate moment nourished the Wizard as he was struck by the wonder of what had happened. His breath steadied to its regular pace, his eyes adjusted to the star crowded sky.

Perched here, he felt the tender breeze return, stroking at his face and licking his arms. His eyes wandered in all directions to get a sense of where his boat now was, the milky breath of stars sprawled in a line across the horizon, while just off to his right, below the centaurs, a beast was rousing before him.

The black would cover the stars, just a little at first, but as it grew the boat began to rock heavier underfoot, leaning down starboard. The monster pulled at the hull, drawing the boat and the ocean into its gut. The Wizard clung to the mast, which was now mostly horizontal and groaning. His eyes caught the glint of white rock and sand that the boat now rested on. The wave inhaled every drop, every fish and nymph as it filled itself in wrath for the man who woke it this night.

He could hear his men clamouring below deck before they appeared, a trail of ants on the deck one by one. He yelled to them "Get below!" knowing they'd not stand a chance if the wave crashed on them directly.

He watched over, his nose caressed by the arching wave, which had now mostly suspended itself in crest. He looked above him, the frozen wave now looked like the great, gaping mouth of a dragon. It's maws salivating and dripping for the inevitable meal.

The Wizard's blood danced electric and his mostly permanent smile now sprung even wider at the sides. His laughter echoed through the emptiness surrounding him, before tickling at the belly of the great wave. The wave crashed, snapping the mast and pummelling him with the contents of an entire ocean. His body clung to his mast, holding her, his dear Magdalena or that which remained of her. The wave swirled and slushed him in fury, he cracked and smashed into the rocks and the sand and then the hull of the boat as it shot to the sky in violent revolt.

He held strong to his splintered wood, as the sea seemed to settle into its surging protest. His legs would not move, and his head spewed blood, ribbons of red threading through the salty water.

She was probably once very beautiful, he thought, as a face appeared before him. Her hair was fair, and her skin was grey much like the moon. Her white dress seemed to sway and float independently from the waves around it. She was tying something around his head, stemming the blood, he thought, before he realised it'd been some time since he last took a breath.

"Am I dead?" he asked the nymph, his eyes calibrating to both water and wonder.

"Yes," her voice sung hoarse. It too, was probably once very beautiful he thought. "But you'll go back".

As she finished tying his head to the mast, several more nymphs swam their slender bodies to his. Some were beautiful, he realised, strikingly so. Others were withered and bitter not unlike the women at home. One, the most beautiful, now held her face in front of his, no more than a few inches away. She too was lit like the moon, but in her, the colour seemed neither pallid nor dreary. Her smile was the most remarkable thing he'd ever seen.

She brought her hands to his face, tenderly cupping his cheeks, and her eyes, green and loving, locked with his. He thought to beg not to return, but felt a tugging and tearing at his legs. He looked down and saw the nymphs stripping the skin from his limbs, his legs now sinew, and broken flesh and bone protruded from his thigh.

"We have to prepare you," the pretty young one said, stroking his face.

"For what?"

"To return." She smiled at him, her gentle face framed by her swirling hair.

"Back there?" He gestured to the surface with his head.

"That's right, dear," she said, as the nymphs bit into his flesh, tearing it with their teeth and spitting it out.

"But … how?" he wondered, his legs now limp. One ankle had been ripped from its socket, floating somewhere near his hand. "How can I sail, like this?"

"Oh no, you'll never sail again," she sang, her voice considerably lighter than the message it delivered.

"But, I am a sailor, that's all I am, I am all that."

"Oh no, dear." She brushed his concerns like a fly over ale. "You're not a sailor."

He froze, suspended and aching as the nymphs continued to tear and pull at his body, destroying it, peeling at each limb and ligament. They are monsters, he thought, but for the beauty that touched his face. His gut now roared and festered, fury rose from within.

"I am a sailor!" he screamed, roaring through the ocean, agonised and desperate. All that he'd built himself to be, all that he was known for, the bread on his plate, that all came from him being a sailor.

And he wasn't just any sailor. He was the best. His legend was known far to the east and north where the sky would dance. Merchants and royals would seek him out to provide safe passage for their goods. He was the greatest, the strongest, a leader of leaders. He would use his nose and skin to navigate when his eyes were shut. He would move the stars to steer the ship when the waves were heavy. He was The Wizard, he thought.

The nymphs kept stripping at his skin, killing him, destroying him, as he writhed to be free from their violence. He shook and flailed, his muscles covered with bite marks and his might gone.

The beauty stroked his eyebrows, her voice soft and singing, like a lyre or a child, lulling him into surrender. It was ambrosia, he thought, as his head swelled and settled in its rhythm.

When he looked back to his legs, the muscles all wasted

and the bronze dulled to grey, his heart shattered with shame. He couldn't go back like this. He couldn't lift a barrel or draw an anchor or command great men. He was all stringy and scarred, his foot, now tied back to his leg, hung limp and turned to the side.

"Much better," the beauty sang as she leant to kiss his mouth. The Wizard was paralysed, broken by the fear of returning like this. As the nymphs swam away, each following another, he felt his anger rise. *Better than what?*

The beauty tugged at his mast, removing it from the silt and sand that had held it in place while they worked. She smiled at him, all serene and magic, her eyes sparkling with the rising sun above. She glowed golden now, as the moon yielded to the dawn, and pushed his mast upward to the surface.

"I can't go back!" he screamed, his body broken and not moving as his mind intended. "I can't be a sailor like this." As his body, broken and lame, floated upward and he surrendered to the agony of a life stripped of the sea, his eyes flashed with a pristine memory of the beautiful nymph.

"You're not a sailor." The words dripped from her tongue like honey or salve. The sun now beamed onto his body as he saw the hull, dark and desperate looming above him.

That's right, he thought. *I'm not a sailor.*

I am The Wizard.

RAISING POSEIDON

"I'm a god."

The Mother fell firm upon the linen, her face so heavy against the damp bedding that her cheek pressed into her nose. It'd been a long labour, the days had bled into nights and this, the third night, was now sinking well into dawn.

She wasn't privy to the discussions outside her room. The village women would sit and sip tea, one and then the other claiming her body too small, her hips too square, too shallow. Their voices struck the walls in procession until the thud of, "she's old and stubborn."

"I'm a god," she said again. This time her knees slipped from underneath her, causing her hips to crash to the bed like an old bridge bearing an army. She felt audacious. It was not at all something she'd normally say, but as she heard the tiny whimper and then a scream of the baby she'd been pushing for days, she felt it to be true. Despite the agony and madness, she'd not strayed from the belief that a baby would soon nestle in her arms. Hope, she believed, was a guiding force far beyond the ephemeral signals of her body.

The midwife held the baby up, its cord pulsing with the potent stream of nourishment from The Mother's fragile body. At that moment, he belonged to two realms: of womb and world; of earth and ether.

"I'm a god." Her mouth sprawled itself across her face. Her statement, while completely audacious, now felt somewhat comfortable falling from her lips. She had just birthed creation, this plump and silvery shining boy.

It was the type of thing that Zeus took great humour in. A mortal woman, collapsed upon her maternal bed, puddled in blood and claiming divinity. Her skin was pale and flushed, sweat gripping her brow. He'd walked in as the physician would, asking the midwife about the baby's vitals and The Mother's health. He'd even peered into her eyes, asking The Mother if she knew what day it was, where she was, if she knew the King. His old hands were cold against her skin as he searched for pulses and pressed upon flesh for signs of blood coursing.

He'd been not much taller than the midwife. At first, she'd noticed his shoulders had been narrow and his shirt buttoned neatly to his throat. But as he was talking to her, his cloudy, blue eyes started to darken as if a storm had spread across them. His face bulged and his jaw pulled heavy, the bone thickening beneath taut skin. His hair, which was combed and slick with oil sitting just above his ears and with a perfect part on his left side, tousled itself into thick waves. What was white beyond the glean of shining marble, now flowed gold and curled to his shoulders.

In the coming days, The Mother would wonder if this were even a memory. While the details were sharp and each time she'd recall them they'd fall in the same, strict sequence, there was also the pooling blood between her thighs, staining her certainty.

Zeus cupped his hands to the baby's cheeks, looking at its tiny face in theatrical approval. "Ohhhh, so darling," he said with his eyes squinted and head askew, much the same as the women that would soon visit. His laughter booming and all in one moment great and elated, while the echoes wandered insincerely. Warmth sunk first from his eyes, and then his mouth and smile seemed to stiffen and harden with disgust. "You call yourself a god?"

It wasn't so much a question, although the way 'god' swept up at the end suggested that he would require her answer. She knew he'd heard her say it; he'd not ask if he wasn't sure. He was always sure.

"No." The word flicked from her mouth and her eyes widened, her tongue surprised by the taste of her won lie. "I mean, I did," she quickly corrected, "but I am not. I am a mortal. I just did a miraculous thing." She'd not intended to conjure wrath, albeit that of Zeus. Her mind had slipped an instant when she'd pushed to birth her son.

"But miracles are of heaven." Boom. Boom. Boom. Each word sounded like the drums before battle as he'd strike fist to palm.

He plucked the baby from the midwife, holding it, his eyes squared to the tender eyelids flickering to open. "Brother!" his laughter hit The Mother with great confusion. Before she could summons a coherent thought, Zeus pursed his lips—

great crimson things with a bow not unlike the mountains of Thraki. A stream of warm, immortal breath bled from his mouth and spiralled its way to the baby's face. Its tiny lungs inhaled the holy puff.

He passed the baby back to the midwife, as though it were just the blanket and no living being breathed within it.

"My brother requires a mother." The corners of his mouth teased at satisfaction, curling themselves up proud and smug.

The Mother knew that Zeus and Poseidon were once again at war. The brothers, as most brothers did, would fight and fracture, each jostling for dominance. Unlike most brothers though, whose rivalry extended to the meal, or land, or maybe women, when Zeus and Poseidon warred the whole earth would shake. Humans would be trampled like ants and mites, people would be moved and played like parts in a tragedy.

The Mother looked back to her baby. He'd been wrapped again in cloth, this time tighter, as though the midwife expected his arms to break free. His eyes, which had before only fluttered against the light, now beamed wide and welled with a Cycladic blue. This was now Poseidon, she thought. She'd committed a cosmic crime by claiming herself *theos* and had now become an accessory to Zeus's deviance. She'd raised herself to the blood of gods, now she must raise a god.

"But I am mortal," The Mother's voice spilled from her mouth as blood spilled to the sheets. To raise Poseidon she thought, was a far greater agony than that of birth. If he were a mortal she'd hold the comfort that any mistake she made would be limited to him, to her family. To raise a god, however, she'd not be afforded even a mundane mistake. Tiny gods with tempers could end civilisations.

Zeus smiled, warm before reaching his hand to touch her foot. "You need some rest," he said tenderly. She watched his bronze hand move across the bed and then being struck by the morning light pouring in from the window. White, she thought. Again, his hand was white. The very-human wrinkled fingers that had prodded at her and checked her pulses now came to rest by her knee.

"Find your strength." He nodded slowly. She watched every rise and fall and his carefully oiled hair with its perfect part on the right. Not a lock would betray him. He turned, his narrow back now facing the midwife, his shoulders almost mirroring hers as he walked to the door.

The Mother woke to darkness and looked over to her baby. His plump skin gleamed in the moonlight. His lips were pink and swollen and not unlike Zeus's, just smaller. His little fingers curled inward, tiny fists clutching at confusion and the sparking delight of this new world. He looked like an ordinary baby, she thought to herself, not knowing what a god baby should look like. She'd only heard that they arrive with great ceremony, as he had.

His eyelids slid upward, and she caught the briefest of peeks of glistening blue eyes. In there, she saw the inhuman; disdain for Zeus and his new mortal life, his gaze stretching far beyond the room.

His mouth gaped now. He looked for milk while The

Mother sat stunned, his lips pursing and suckling, ready for breast. She still sat stunned. *This is not my baby*, she thought, *that is not my baby.*

Poseidon, in all of his craving, now screamed for his feed, his lungs driving air with a strength unheard of in mortal babies. The pitch seemed to squeal and pierce right through The Mother's ears. Grating at her tensions and coursing blood to her legs, ready to run.

Though she knew little of gods, she knew even less of motherhood. Her own mother had felt the role a burden and sent her to live with The Crone, who watched her more than she guided. The Crone's eye would glint and shine in awe as the child would grow under her watch. The Crone, in all of her wisdom and for some part laziness, knew that the fates would be told in the way that they wish, and little, be it guardian or gold, could interfere with that. There were too many heroes born of the dust and too many monsters born of a crown.

As The Mother bloomed, and her body unfurled from the awkward binding of childhood, she took to poppy and wine. At feasts she would laugh and sing, louder than the other women, sitting on the knees of generals and soldiers. Her fun was greatly unfettered, and her legs would wrap around the bodies of strangers.

The Crone, although not entirely the voyeur, had found her own licentiousness spilling from the girl. She'd sit, air still in her lungs, waiting for the inevitable crash of reality coming the girl's way. Lessons could not be taught so swiftly, nor so deftly as those that come from experience. The wine and the poppy, the men and the parties, would one day surely sour. The Crone relished her part in this.

It had come, almost unexpectedly although quite inevitably, after the harvest feast. The girl had been philandering with a soldier who was to head south with his unit in the morning. They'd spent hours together in his tent, drinking and playing. He'd asked her to leave as the afternoon yielded to dusk, and as she did, the wine soured in her belly. Her heart ached for a husband, a lover who wouldn't leave come dawn. She'd taken sick for days as The Crone fed her broth and herbs.

It was amongst the herb, the violet sea of thyme and sage on the hill that she met her husband. He herded goats there but had land with crops and honey in the valley. She'd never cared for farmers before, much less goat herders. They smelled of the animals they kept, and they kept time to the season. She'd always preferred the smell of brutality, or war or wild merchant, erratic and untethered. Perhaps it was the sea air pregnant with thyme, or her bare feet upon rock anchoring her to the slow, inevitable cycle of life. She felt safe, held even, with the barest of looks from him.

Her bosom had only filled in the days before birth. She'd been tending to her body, sick as it was, with food and rest and offerings for Artemis and Demeter, yet her belly had barely grown. At least, she thought, *my birth will be easy*.

The Mother sat up, wriggling her body and dropping her gown to feed the howling child. He latched at her breast and suckled so strongly that it fell flat in an instant. Again, he howled, the screech not human, not animal.

"I'm just a mortal!" she cried again. This time the midwife, who had been soaking a cloth in herbs, raised just one eye toward The Mother.

"You seek the easy path?" It was clearly not a question.

"No, I seek the right path, for me," The Mother answered in protest, her voice cracked like a child being scorned and not fed. She'd watched other women birth and raise their children, it seemed undoubtedly easy as you wrapped them and fed them and prayed that their hearts wouldn't stop.

"And who are you to know the right path?" Again, a question that wasn't a question.

"I know that my life is simple. And he is not."

The midwife slid her hand under the baby's head, lifting it and wrapping it in linen before pulling at The Mother's gown and setting Poseidon to the other breast. This time, he suckled gently and seemed to drift off to sleep.

"Do you seek for this to be gone?"

"No!" Disgust now shot from her tongue unguarded. She'd heard about midwives and their offerings, be it to a god or sovereign or the barren wives of merchants.

"Then you seek for greater strength."

The Mother's cheeks flushed, shame crawling through her capillaries. Beyond the agony of birth, she'd never much considered her need for further strength. When she broke from the poppy and mended her heart of the soldier, she had crafted her life to be one of value. She'd deal in herbs at the agora and teach others to tend to their wounds. She was the wife of a landholder, and he was nice enough, strong and with wit that would crack like a whip when aroused. They'd tend to crops of grape and olive, milk goat and made cheese.

It was wholly the land that anchored her here. The tactile delight of rubbing thyme between her fingers, the aroma filling the air and drawing her feet further into the earth's embrace. It struck her at times the difference she'd felt in her being from when she'd tinkered with ambrosia. All that time she'd sought to be beyond her limbs, beyond her thoughts, floating in the abyss where gods would frolic.

That was her strength, she thought, when the midwife questioned her. She'd settled nicely into that life, her senses guiding her, comforts splayed in all directions. While they were not among the richest of families, they couldn't want for more.

And yet here she was, seeking more. Of something she'd not identified while its light beamed upon her inadequacies. She writhed and squirmed, Poseidon now asleep at her breast and the thought flushing her mind was, if she made a mistake with him, the earth would shake.

Had she always settled for the easy path? The life of tilling soil and tending to gardens, her fingernails stained with dirt and grape and calloused by the miracle that next season, she'd need to do it all again. Her life was quite hard enough, she thought to herself.

It was not her duty nor her passion to raise a god. Zeus's quarrel should not stretch its arms to her. She wanted to summon him and beg for his mercy. For him to blow the same breath that filled her son with Poseidon's blood and have her baby back the same.

"I need to speak to Zeus."

The midwife's eyes shifted upward to the corner of the room, pausing a moment before rolling over the mother, scanning her for lucidity.

"To speak to gods you must first win their favour." A small laugh scurried from her throat.

"I need to speak to Zeus!" Her voice now stretched and scraped like a blade upon rock. Her womb felt like carrion being devoured by vultures, clamping it in their talons.

She was not a god. This was not for her. This was not fair, or right, or just or fated.

"You'll never raise a child when you're acting like one."

The Mother sat cold, the words tearing her from her tantrum. How dare she, she thought, a hired hand! The realisation soon flickered that this woman had led hundreds of women into motherhood. The voice trickled coarse through her thoughts—'you're acting like one'—it seemed to settle and shame her in the same breath.

She awoke with the baby beside her. He was wrapped in wool cloth, the midwife must have tended to him as the night sunk to the earth, cool and wet with the wind from the sea. His tiny body was still asleep, his chest rising and then dropping in an ebb and flow like the waves he would one day rule. He was so precious here, beyond her fears and the torment of what the future would bring. She brought her hand to his juicy little cheeks and allowed herself the slightest of smiles to be carved to her face. She cupped her fingers, his soft skin creamy and silken beneath the pads of her callouses.

He trembled a little, startled. The Mother wondered if it were a dream, or the sliding of his awareness into this new form. *Does he know who he is?* She wondered when any baby would begin to know himself beyond the needs for food and sleep and love.

The midwife returned, her hands stacked with neat squares of clean cloth, wool and linen both. "You had a good sleep," she said, knowing in her experience that the most fearful ones tended to feel peace after sleep. She pulled at the blanket, and blood seeped through as she packed cloth soaked in herbs between The Mother's thighs. "Rest up dear."

The Mother was unsure if it was the sight of her own blood or the amount she had lost that was tending her to weakness. Her tongue taste of metal, and her mouth dried and clicked as she tried to talk. The midwife had seemingly known this, as she held a cup of warm tea to The Mother's mouth, dripping the honey steeped herbs as The Mother shook, chilled. The doors had been open while The Mother slept, the midwife stood to shut them.

"Leave them," The Mother said, gesturing for more tea. "I like the sound." The ocean whooshed, embryonic, in the distance.

"I don't want the easy path." The Mother raised, wanting to apologise for her tantrum prior but feeling the blood slipping from her veins. She felt weakened now, beyond that which she'd ever felt from the poppy. She felt her body soaking into the bed around her, her energy slipping and spilling from the veins it should have been coursing.

When she woke, again, the baby was crying. The midwife was rummaging in her tunic, pulling at The Mother's breast as though it were an instrument or tool. The Mother watched in awe, as the midwife held the baby balanced on two fingers, the other hand pulling at the breast and then pushing Poseidon to the nipple. She was amazed at the dexterity and also the feeling that this was no longer her breast. It felt different now, no longer a part of her to display her fertility, her ample heaving lust.

Poseidon gulped, again in one overwhelming mouthful, flattening The Mother's breast. This was the god, she realised, the almighty and immortal, drinking of her. He screamed, again, the inhuman and excruciating squeal, as though he'd been starved through the ages, lifetimes searching for food.

The Mother's eyes twinkled now, her ears warmed, and her throat seemed to swell with the rising grip of sadness. As the midwife shuffled the boy to the other breast, his tongue pulled on a long thread The Mother had never before known, each suckle ripping the cord to her womb, knotting it, squeezing it in an agony not unlike birth.

The Mother felt her legs warm and wet, as blood further spilled from her groin. She felt her eyes melting into the darkness behind their sockets. Her head sinking and floating at once, drifting between this world and ether.

"I don't want the easy path," she called somewhere to the corner of the room. Mostly, it had been her fractured ego that needed to assert itself, but beneath the splintered remains was a quiet realisation that this was indeed a gift. Zeus picked her. She, the chosen.

"My dear, you're going to have to find strength." The midwife gripped The Mother's shoulder, shaking it, hoping to rouse her back.

"My dear?" The midwife's face was now mere inches from The Mother's.

"I have nothing," The Mother slurred, each word rolling into the next and mostly indistinguishable from the last.

"You need nothing, my dear, just a desire for life."

The Mother drifted back to her crop. The hills rolling with a gentle undulation she'd never before noticed. The harsh crags now softened and brushed with grass and wild wheat. Though she thought it was well past summer, the tender bleating of baby goats called through the hills, the bucks watching from above. Colour had burst here, she felt, her memories never so vivid as the scent of island thyme soaked her nose.

She lay down, the grass lush and soft beneath her. The warm air caressed her face as the sun filled the sky with a golden orb. She breathed fully, orgasmically, basking in the ripe fig and apricots that fondled the air.

Here, she was nothing. The expanse of sky stretching above her, the earth beneath her, all reminding her of her supreme nothingness. She'd not really considered herself a nothing before, her days swept in a haze of her own self-importance. But now, sinking in bliss, she felt a complete, exquisite nothing. The grass could swallow her, and the world would still turn, the sun and stars gliding as they do.

There was something remarkable beyond that which she knew. The brilliant intelligence of creation, calling the bird to sing, calling the seed to break soil, calling the heart to beat. She was nothing, even in her reverence tending to crops, feeding her goats or soaking leaves in wine for medicine. She was nothing, and if the soil she lay upon swallowed her here, not much would change.

She felt her body empty of all that had weighted it. All the stories of who she was and what she knew, all the stories of what gods do and do not like. All the brittle incidences that chipped at her heart. The stream of her soul dampened the soil around her as she became one brilliant nothing.

In the distance, she heard a child's voice. Not quite singing, but ethereal, nonetheless. It warbled lightly as the words dripped and danced. Each line calling her to join in, for her to follow and respond.

O' Divine Mother,
Rain on me your love
Hold me, when I cannot hold myself
Show me the way to forgiveness, of myself, and of others
Show me the way to love, for I too, am that,
Flood the light of your grace through me
So that others may be filled
Cradle me in this world of contrasts,
Where light can appear dark
And likewise the darkness light
O' Divine Mother,
Share with me your wisdom
So that I may know what's right
Share with me your courage
So within what's right I act
And share with me your stillness
So that I may hear your voice
O' Divine Mother,
It is through loving you,
That I may learn to love me,
Fully,
Eternally.

The sun beamed heavier now, and the wind picked up around her, the grass flattening in its gust. She noticed the goats, the buck on the hill, now shaking and stumbling as the rock seemed to fall underneath him. She felt it too, the earth shaking and trembling, a violent collapse beneath her. The colours that had been so rich now bled to grey and her eyes shut heavy.

She felt the midwife pushing honey to her lips.

"Swallow." Her voice held a power beyond men. The Mother did so, feeling the sugar pulse through her blood and her head seemed to settle. Poseidon slept, his breath rising and falling, ebbing and flowing. The ocean, that he will one day rule, she thought.

"You woke him." The midwife smiled, as though relaxed or relieved.

"But he sleeps," said The Mother, logic finally snapping in a congruent thought.

"Not him," she gestured the baby, "the god, Poseidon."

The Mother pressed two fingers between her eyebrows, sliding them over her forehead. Pockets of memories that ought not be together, entwined themselves in her mind.

"When you prayed, he stirred. When he stirred, so did the earth."

The Mother leant to her child, feeling her nothingness return with an overwhelming everything. The umbilical cord of Mother God pulsing a potent stream of nourishment through her.

The Mother pulled her newborn close and whispered

softly in his ear, "I seek not the easy path, but the strength to raise a god."

OF BREATH AND FIRE

When his nostrils twitched that way, they knew he was moments from rage. They seemed to pulse and beat and pull at the worn tendons that clamped his jaw shut. To anyone else, the flaring may have gone unnoticed, or been dismissed as a tick or reference to the music, but the musicians were tuned to his every gesture, every nuanced expression, and knew that fury would soon follow.

This day, it was the flautist, a young woman who had made the ridiculous decision to speak when he raised the subject of her sloppy playing. "This is just practice, sir." The other players sunk further into their seats, for her, and what would follow. It mostly fascinated them, the arrival of someone new, watching them assert themselves, defend themselves, blood flushing their faces and sweat gripping their fingers. For many, once was enough to be torn apart by The Maestro, they'd be wise enough or stupid enough to watch the others in their section and nod or sink when he would chastise.

The Flautist seemed not to have grasped this concept. This was her third round of abuse in just as many days. Her spine would stay straight, traced by the length of her hair that dropped below the seat of her chair. Her neck was long which further infuriated The Maestro, her head bobbing ripe for the slaughter.

"Practice," he said in a laboured attempt at calmness, "is for home." His voice rose and his mouth grew wider with each word that followed the last, every syllable stretching like a net cast over and around her. "Do not waste my time. This is rehearsal."

The girl seemed dull, or perhaps she was strong. She spoke again, this time apologising when all others would have bowed their head, hiding tears or blood flushed faces. "Sorry, sir." It felt at once sincere but also unbothered, as though his words had been received by an equal.

"You'd need not apologise if you were better." This time his voice was steady, no anger, just the sting of resentment upon his tongue.

He loathed them. Every one of them. He'd watch them play with their clumsy fingers moved by memory and not by the music. Their faces were frozen as they read the notes, looking to him for meaning and feeling.

He knew every note, every pause, every break with intimacy. He'd spend his days exploring the crevices within a score, holding the distance between cello and horn in outstretched fingers, his palms weighted with sound.

Over the years resentment had thickened upon him, his skin stiffened, and lines would be carved into his brow and lips such that disappointment rest upon him always. His eyes tended toward a squint, as though he had to squeeze his vision to fathom another's stupidity.

He'd sought perfection, which seemed quite an obvious thing to do, yet many conductors merely did their best. His job, he believed, relied upon the precise transmission of the composer's message. To do otherwise would simply reduce the meaning, a misrepresentation. His purpose was to honour and devote himself to its delivery.

Momentarily, he'd be cupped in perfection. His musicians would yield to his baton and eyes, their lessons all so entwined in their fingers that they could forget them and submit to his waving hand or a nod or a pause. The veil of thought would be dropped, his players each abandoning the rules or traumas they'd collected and spill into the slipstream of concert.

The Maestro lathered himself in those moments. He'd live for them, gearing himself toward more, and more, and more. When the sound moved contrary, he'd fly into a rage, sometimes violently and stands or chairs or instruments would be strewn across halls into faces or feet. He could not understand how people could bear being happy in mediocrity, especially submerged in art.

Parenthood, he thought, that's the place for mediocrity. With messy children crying and emitting all kinds of fluids. Where the precise moment could not be judged in perfection, as boys would take years to become men. The parent could sit in complacency hoping that their disinterest might yield a hero. He'd never bothered himself with such abysmal tasks, he had no interest in children as a legacy; his name would live on through music.

He'd barely gotten halfway through the first movement

when breath stung the air and his ears. The Flautist, again, in another clumsy buckle inhaled in the moments before her part. It was short and mostly silent, but The Maestro was shot with disruption.

This time he seethed silently, his front teeth grinding as he tried to dive back into the symphonic waves. He'd sit, close to the crest but the waves pummelled and his composure was lost. They'd played it right, but it wasn't perfect. Their best was not his best.

"Leave," he said, his voice booming as the entire orchestra swept their eyes to the ground so as not to catch his wrath. The Flautist, in innocence and foolery, looked at him directly as she tried to apologise with her eyes. "Leave!" he spat, louder this time.

Swiftly they moved from the concert hall, all but The Flautist who dithered and looked to The Maestro as he walked to the door. She'd wanted direction more so than approval—she wanted to please him and perform with the perfection he sought. Yet the notes on her page would not allude to his requirements. His need for specificity would not extend to his explanations or pandering to those who took the time to learn.

He leant over the stovetop, stirring the cold soup as the hob glowed beneath it. It still smelled okay, he thought, as it began to waft through the kitchen. The cat, who'd been asleep and would stay asleep, stirred briefly. This had been its bed for some time now, its ribs rippling through tabby fur. Occasionally it would get up forgetting its frailty and run for the door before its legs would buckle and piss would pool on the linoleum.

He cleared his throat, the rasps of resentment catching and splaying his cheeks while his nostrils lifted their skirts to show the darkened airway within. He'd not always felt like this, there'd been a great deal of time that he held a real joy for the craft. After he left the conservatoire, and in those first appointments, he'd had little expectation for himself. He'd learn to venerate perfection, as the boy yielded to the coarse strictures of man. He'd feel his glory growing, the myth of his excellence. They'd no longer talk about the motherless stump of a boy, the kid and his ragged clothes, the disappointment for his father, the composer.

They began instead to discuss their memories of great composers, and his name was spread against theirs. He'd barely felt that as a child; even before his mother left, she'd hardly been warm. But here, in the perpetual pursuit of perfection, he felt adored.

He vaguely remembered that boy, and his days at the conservatoire. It had been mostly a delight, as he'd stretch out on beds and entertain women. The conservatoire always had an abundance of women spilling from its halls, like the juice of ripe plums squeezed between fingers. He'd pick and pluck the best and explore their warmth and crevices. Mostly they wanted to be seen as musicians of some sort. It was still rare if not frowned upon for women to preside in orchestras.

It was quite the contrast; the life he pursued and the life he enjoyed in dormitories or gardens or parties. The fleshy surprise and excitement of the women as he'd trace the lines of their hips, the curves of their waists, listening to their breaths beg hollow then full. It was chaos in the most glorious way. Some would grasp his hand and place it exactly where they wanted, some would put their hand exactly where he wanted, and others would lay timid while he explored at will.

But when he raised his baton, that would all fade. His eyes would narrow and his ears would widen to capture the pulse of his orchestra's heart. He'd become rigid, his lips strung together in stitches that would give no emotion. Each note, each rest, would be as the composer wrote it, without exception.

As he reached the final year of his studies, his reputation bulged and discussions with his teachers turned to not if, but where, he would be appointed. That word, again, almost carved in him a hollow. Perfect, they would say. Perfect, as though it were a diamond or ruby and shall always remain.

With appointments came applause, with applause came expectation. The more he'd be stained with perfect the more the gravity bore down on him. He'd feel pulled to maintain their assumptions and then more. Within him festered a need to be more perfect, to gain greater acclaim, greater appointments, greater stages. He'd pore over each work, dissecting and inhaling every score. He'd look for the composer's sentiment, for every breath taken while the music was written. Obsession burned through him as the women and parties slid away.

The thing with perfection, that Maestro failed to realise for much too long, was that once it was there, it just hung there. It didn't really do much. It didn't breathe or dance, it didn't drink or eat. Its leaves didn't drop in the winter to return in the spring. It didn't bask in the sunlight and hide in the dark. Its jaw clamped shut and its limbs strung to torso.

His audiences began to bore of him. The appointments that once flooded from the finest houses in the finest cities now trickled from only outlying theatres and halls. He'd blame them, the renegades and the young, their disrespect and disregard for the craft of composition. They'd take liberties and stretch the chords, take rests where there were none. And the composers began to parade like peacocks, their faces lit and responsive as though they danced with the music, instead of commanding it.

Audiences soaked in the heresy. They delighted in the choruses and anticipation. One conductor stood one night, for minutes or more, gilded with applause mid-score before returning to the programme. The crescendo had built so greatly, and the crowds so familiar with the work that he just rested there, holding suspense as a ball in his hand, waiting for the crowd to embed their breath and ecstasy into the house. They built the crest, he played. He'd allowed them into the orchestra, as players and participants. Every clap, every astonished gasp, every wide-mouthed grin, feeding the crescendo until it broke. Orchestral orgasm, he called it.

The Maestro was done when iconoclasts would line the stage where professionals once stood. He'd built himself an armour with his stranglehold on perfection. He'd let nobody in, not the orchestra, not the audience. He couldn't linger in the unknown as did his contemporaries. He'd find it excruciating, even in practice. The score had been written, and it was his job to service it.

Then, there was that woman. The one who breathed. The one who spoke. It was not entirely unusual for him to have women amongst his players these days. As the great appointments dried up so too did the men willing to play with him. He'd be bombarded with auditions of women desperate for a chance to play on a real stage. Mostly they were quite good and didn't seem to despise him in the way the men now did. There was something about a reputation that could celebrate or slaughter a man. Men tended to adopt reputation as their own opinion well before a woman would. The women would watch him writhe in fury when the symphony was coarse, and pity him or show sympathy. He couldn't quite tell the difference, but at least they'd not quit as the men did.

He'd barely sat down to eat when a trickling rap at the door interrupted his mouthful. The soup had been warmed but not quite through, the potatoes and meat still cold inside. He detested interruptions and did not understand why people insisted upon blurring the lines of professionalism. There was work, and there was home. Nobody need visit him at home.

The timid knock came once more, followed by a familiar inhale and, "Sir?" That voice he thought, his blood simmering. He'd had propositions before and always denied them vehemently. These desperate creatures that craved acclaim, each looking for a foothold to bolster their fractured esteem.

The only way to receive such acclaim was to work hard and show dedication.

"Sir, I brought fresh bread." Her voice was unlike others that had come before, she seemed confident, and her neck stretched high with contentment. His face screwed in confusion, trying to understand her angle. Usually, they offered their bodies, he smirked, if he were tender to bribery it would be a slow route using sticks of bread. "My husband is a baker."

"And he allows you to play?" The Maestro's tongue stung with judgement as he questioned the woman.

She laughed. "He's usually sleeping now." She understood the sentiment of elders, her parents too astonished by the liberties women would take. "But yes, he allows me."

The Maestro was grabbed by the way she said 'allows.' He circled it, looking for a reference that would satisfy his ageing understanding. Something within suggested that it had not been a verbal grant of permission, but a more general expectation of their marriage.

"How can I help you?" he asked, his words seeking to be rid of the girl, more than his manners suggested.

"I just want to apologise—" she started, her voice stained with the obvious realisation that she had no idea what she was apologising for.

"No need, just practice more," he said, glad to have settled it.

"What do you recommend I practice?" she asked, naive to the old man's desire for solitude.

"Everything. Start with your scales … and your breathing. Is that all?"

The words had hardly left his mouth when an agonising screech came from the corner of the room. The wall began to pound and scratch with a strict rhythm that startled The Maestro. His face peeled of colour, now ivory gloss like the keys of a piano.

"The cat!" he said, looking stupefied and incompetent. He never knew what to do with it when it shook so violently. Its limbs would stretch and lock and it would rock as though possessed. He turned from the door, stepping back into the kitchen and meaning for the girl to leave, but she followed him.

He stood beside the cat, his instincts imploring him to commit to aid, but his head froze him with questions.

"It's fitting," the girl said, her knees dropping beside the pillow and blanket in the corner of the kitchen. Her hand moved to its chest, palm resting across its heart and slender fingers gently stroking in a gesture intended to calm.

"Is it okay?" he asked, his head looking around the woman to see the cat now settling.

"No. I don't think so. How often does it happen?"

"It used to be only occasionally, but the last couple of days it's happened a lot." The Maestro's voice had dropped all of its formalities, the brittle arrogance now yielding to confused humility. "It's not my cat," he added. "It was here when I got here." He felt defensive, protective, as though he were saying it to prove he would be above allowing a cat to become ill, had it been in his care always.

The fitting stopped as the cat cried and its paws softened to a tremble, electricity striking its nerves as its body discharged the residues of spasm. It purred for a moment before melting still.

"It's gone," The Flautist said with grief extending beyond her knowledge of the cat.

The Maestro returned to his chair to finish his soup, realising that he had to implement a greater strategy for her to leave.

"Are you okay?" she asked, her eyes speckled pink and glassy.

"Yes, fine," he answered, his mind focused on polite ways to get her to leave.

"Would you like for me to wrap it?"

"Wrap what?" he asked, impatience grinding at his manners.

"The cat, sir. It's dead."

The Maestro cocked his head to one side, certain that just moments ago she had said the fit had passed. "The cat's dead?"

"It is, sir."

He stood, walking to the cat as though in disbelief. The Flautist moved aside as he knelt beside the animal, his wits dulled to understanding. He touched its leg. It's still warm, he thought. He deftly sought to ridicule the girl, before sensing something greater gone. The leg, while warm and twitching, felt empty and whole all at once. As though death was full within it, and life had drifted above.

The Maestro reached beneath its body and lifted it as he stood up. His face was now flushed of reason, and the need for action stiffened in his skin. He moved across the kitchen, desperation for purpose carving his muscles to carry the animal somewhere and do something. He headed toward the door hoping to toss the thing in the brambles next door but saw the twinkling glints of moonlight catching on falling mist, so instead placed the cat upon the bin by the sink.

She watched him fumble, in awe. The lines on his face being forced toward strength, or the perception of such. When he'd knelt to gather the tabby body in his arms, it had seemed almost tender, loving. But following that, his mouth pursed and his head tilted back, his nose rising to the sky as his eyes looked downward. To others, it would appear arrogant, but to her, she saw the grips of control desperately seeking a purchase where confusion reigned.

He'd not dealt with death before, he had a bird as a child but he'd not known for years that it had died. He'd been told it flew away, with great poetry of its journey to the equator and all its stops upon the way. It was his mother, before she left, that one day told him it had been a lie, that she woke one morning to find it dead in the cage. He'd dealt with the loss long ago, but something new tugged at him, like deception or mystery or filth.

Since his tenure at the conservatoire, he'd mostly avoided people anyway. If they'd have keeled he'd not have ached or mourned. But this cat, the cat he was to care for, struck in him such a confusion, a contradiction of duty and sorrow spanning his body and spilling into the kitchen.

"I could light a pyre," she offered as he sat back at his soup and slurped at the cold broth. His eyes fixed on the table, wide as though his stretched eyelids would allow the extra space his thoughts required.

"It's just a cat," he answered, amused by the girl's sentimentality.

"Well, you can't leave it there." Her head dropped to one side and she gestured the bin. "And wolves still come this far for sheep."

The Maestro gave his automatic look of cynicism. He wore this most regularly when dealing with people, especially women. A wolf will not open his door, he thought, holding in a chuckle. Not long after he realised that he couldn't leave the cat here, in the kitchen. Roaches and rats would come to feast as its body festered and rotted and stiffened and stank. If he left it outside it would indeed invite wolves, and the village was scarred deep from the tales of children and babies taken at dusk.

He thought beyond the unnecessary and excessive display of ceremony, the mechanics of a pyre would be suitable. The body would no longer be, its flesh would fall to ash amongst branches and coal.

"Okay," he replied, slurping again in a display that alluded to soup steaming and hot, as though to temper it for his lips. It was clumsiness though, as he settled himself into this girl taking the reins.

Her eyes fell on him, heavy, as her lips thinned and pressed together in a thin line of pink. What was that? He shuffled in the seat, catching her gaze and immediately turning away. Pity? Remorse? Disgust?

She watched this brittle man, so filled with duty and structure and immersed in his stew that smelled a day past good. She sensed within him a sadness or grief, not for the cat, but the part of himself that felt. He couldn't have always been this way. While she'd heard stories of his father—one of the great composers—and she imagined his diligence spilling into his son, there must have been a moment in his youth where he played and laughed and lingered in song and warmth.

"Do you have a lamp?" she asked. The moon now beamed full and silver and filled the sky with light and shadow too, but the clouds sprawled across the night and would soon slip over its glow.

He pointed to the bench near the window. A large ring of keys sat brassed with an authority The Maestro so dearly attained. His baton, too, sat beside it and reminded her of his devotion to work. Her eyes drifted sideward, wandering around the room as she looked for a picture or pin, or memory of a sweetheart. Nothing. Books of scores stacked high in a phallic gesture to his craft, a single cup and plate. Single knife and fork.

She reached for the lantern and matches beside, pulling at the chimney and setting the wick. The slurping had stopped now, and she turned to catch a glimpse of the man frozen in piety or thought. His eyes set to the wall beyond, his breath steady and rhythmic. Did he even realise she was here? She tried to fuse her visions to picture him enjoying his evening, or lamenting his loss. It all seemed a stretch, and she settled on him sitting in such a way regardless of death or visitors, or success or hardship.

As she opened the door, the cool wisps of wind circled her dress. Winter was warming now, its grip loosening as the days grew longer and the snow dissolved underfoot. She loved this time of year, she could still slip into the night as her husband slept and breathe the crisp air, still look to the stars as they'd dance across the sky and greet each other briefly, before moving on. She'd not need the lamp yet, as she kept it low and beside her knees, but as the wind would rise she'd need it higher to light the narrow path.

Paddocks rolled beyond the theatre. When winter collapsed into spring and the grass dried from the snow, the sheep would be brought up here to graze in emerald fields. They'd birth and nurse, lambs would frolic as gentle breezes would caress the grass, fooling them into jumping higher than the ground beneath. But now, only the soft and occasional shoots of grass would stick up from the cold earth, ice still lingered in parts around trees or rocks where the sun would be shaded even on the warmest days.

The ground crunched and cracked beneath her feet, the brittle remnants of a long winter. The track stretched from the back of the theatre in what was probably once a straight line, but the wear of human feet and the gentle roll of the land now saw it meandering softly to the small hut that was piled with wood. The community had gathered early in autumn to cut wood and build its shelter. Such was the way with the villagers, everything was built as a family.

She began lifting wood, every piece rough and promising to splinter in her hands. She moved it to the paddock below, piece after piece after piece after piece until she'd made a mound from the heaviest up to kindling.

"I'm just going to grab a few things from home," she said, seeing that he'd now washed his plate but sat still in the same chair she'd left him. "And my husband will wake soon," she said. The Maestro was sipping brandy and either had no care that she was there or was burying his thoughts deep in the glass.

"Okay," he said. He seemed happy for her to leave. Her lips thinned again, and her head fell to the side, seeing him as not a man but a boy that was broken and frozen and lone.

When she returned, he was still sitting in the same seat, although the brandy now sunk well beneath half of the bottle's capacity. His mouth wrapped around a pipe, and he puffed as though he were one of the psychoanalysts that people would visit in cities. He looked so curated, like an archetype or character from a novel about a man that was very important to the government or a company he owned. But his eyes fell empty, longing, lonely, or lifeless as though the tendrils of brandy had now reached into his soul and siphoned the residues of vigour.

"It's ready," she said, breaking the air and his paralysis with her silken words. He looked up, he hadn't heard the door or her footsteps which prodded his belief that he was attuned to sound and surrounds with a whip stinging intimacy.

He didn't wish to move, he thought. He didn't understand why he must attend the funeral for a cat that wasn't his and that he'd known for less than a month. But the woman's energy seemed to hook him and lured him to witness the cremation she'd prepared.

He moved like a rock, slow and weighted by the half bottle of brandy. His legs pushing mighty to raise himself from the chair, his palms flat on the table to steady his rock. She'd been tying, tenderly, the cat wrapped in linen. Wormwood and lavender bound to the body, which seemed so big just hours before but was now a tiny parcel. She looked to him, her eyes and gentle smile wordlessly asking if he was ready. He cleared his throat and put down his pipe, reluctant but obliging.

Fire gripped at the clouds as he followed her down the path to the paddock. She'd burned through much of the kindling, and now the larger blocks were starting to catch. The clouds, still coy with the moon, hung low as if shy to swallow its light. Stars washed the sky with milk, and the cold air slapped at his face as though it demanded him sober.

She stood before the fire, her arms stretched in offering as she held the cat to the night and its darkness. His ears, in all their hyper-vigilance, could not make out the whispers slipping from her tongue. She knelt, head bowed and cat held high, before standing once more and turning her head to his for some kind of sign that he was ready.

Nothing. He stood, his eyes now wild and mystified by

this woman that played the flute so poorly. This was her, he thought. This was her element. The flames bursting light onto her skin, golden and beaming against the black backdrop of night. Here, she was perfect. She nodded her head toward the pyre, letting him know that she would now start. He nodded back, mesmerised.

The Flautist now moved toward the fire, placing the cat atop the perch she'd made for its final rest. The flames moved beneath, swaying and popping with the herbs as the wood blackened and fell. Embers leapt from the fire and shot upward, outward, glowing brightly before they vanished. The cat rested upon the coals, each red and furious and The Flautist again, bowed her head, her soft braids somewhat relieved of the duties of the day.

Beside her, was a bag that he'd not noticed. He felt the jarring interruption, here he was waiting, watching, biding his time until the flames dampened and it would be okay to leave. But she pulled out a tin of resin and sprinkled it over the flaming body. Smoky plumes swam like fish to the sky, and the slap of frankincense hit his nose. There was a tenderness here, he thought, in all of the unnecessary and the excess. His mind wandered to his mother when he was young before his father drank and fell into rage. Before she was exhausted and strangled by the composer's explicit demands of purity and piety and sacrifice and strictures.

Singed hair filled the air. The resin and herbs yielded to the stench of animal flesh. Cinders and sinew, crashing, colliding. She brought out her flute and began to play a hymn he'd once known but time and arrogance had swept away. It was perfect, he thought, to play such a song now. His shoulders softened into the ceremony and warmed to her taming the chaos.

There. It broke his thought, not immediately, but obviously and eventually. A few notes had passed before a spark ignited in his thoughts, desperate for attention. There. And there. Hours before he'd been livid with such a blunder, but here in the majesty of ritual, he'd heard her breath all anew. The sensuous inhale before she'd nestle her lips to her flute and shut her eyes to play.

Not *perfect*. Holy.

BETWEEN
✦ TONGUE AND ✦
TOOTH

The Snake wriggled in his seat, the wood beneath him cold and hard. While the chairs would never be called comfortable, today he felt the discomfort grinding. His neck grew hot and sticky, and he was sure his face must be flushed scarlet, a bulb of rubied skin glowing as both target and trophy.

They'd coordinated this, in a big, ugly gesture of their disdain. Ordinarily, the mess hall would have empty tables to spare, and The Snake could always find a corner far from the bustle of service—far from the other boys and their snickers. Today, they'd spread out so that every bench was occupied. Rather than stacking their laughter from a central table, now it echoed throughout the hall.

In doing so, they'd forced him to sit with two other boys that sat opposing each other in the middle of the splintering table. Even with his cheeks tracing the margin of his seat, he was still too close to them. He could smell the horse and rugby mixed with hard soap and a cold shower. He could hear them as they tried so hard to act normal as if they'd been sitting there always. These boys had seemed the least brutish—at least, he'd thought when he'd sat down. Now he was questioning his strategy. In his experience, the weakest ones tended to be the greatest monsters. He wished he'd sat at the table with the boys who had the broadest chests.

Peas rolled across the table to him as he realised these two were probably much simpler than he'd given them credit. If this would be the extent of their torment, it barely scraped his sides. He waited for part two of their assault, eyes scurrying from table to table collecting every morsel of a nod, wink, or anything to prime him to run. For this to be their stunt seemed too easy, too void of the violence they'd mostly opted for. His ears pricked but all he could hear was the slurping of soup and meat being chewed with mouths open wide.

Perhaps that was the point, he thought, thinking maybe these Neanderthals had sparked a new brain cell between them and now watched him writhe. That's what he'd do, he thought, if he were to spend six years stuck in hell with boys he despised. He'd set them up for fear and terror but never let them have it. They'd go mad, he thought, their eyes constantly darting left to right and right to left as they held their necks low between their shoulders, their ears tuned to every word or step.

He could never do that, he thought, set them up for terror. He had his chance when he first came and word of his expulsion in the school down south trailed behind him. He'd been such a mystery to them, he could have twisted their minds in any way he chose.

"I heard he killed a boy," one of the many said just loud enough for him to hear, as though tempting confirmation. They'd done that, at the start, for the first couple of weeks after he arrived. Buffered their comments so as not to excite him, entice him to react erratic, taunt them or draw attention. Over time, they watched him, his silence and sinking posture, his hiding behind lockers and showering alone. Their whispers became louder, a test, or initiation in the place of their regular beating, until one day one boy addressed him directly.

"I heard you killed a boy," he asked, nerves strumming like a slack guitar, his voice quivering and low.

His face got hot as they'd stood around him, there was a group, twenty, maybe thirty bodies crowding him, taking his air, taking his path to the door. He knew he had to say something but as in most of these occasions, actual words wouldn't ripen on his tongue.

"Ahhhh-I... I.... thsssthsssthsss." The sounds hissed and spit as his lips stretched to make something they could recognise.

Their faces all shone as the sun struck them from the window. They looked dazed, swallowed firstly by his attempt to answer and then by what he had answered with. They looked at each other, searching for the protocol for such an event. Their faces smashed with confusion as they reconciled the stories with his response. Were these the words of a killer? They'd never met a killer before, well, at least not a cold-blooded murderer. Many of their teachers had fought in the war and shot men as they were instructed, but given the choice, they'd never just kill.

At some point, a voice from near the back slapped the air with a brittle chuckle. It had broken softly, hidden and short, but it was enough for the others to see his reaction and know that there was no danger. The laughs spawned, blooming like the rot on an apple, spreading across the classroom and through the hall.

"Thsss… thssss… thssss," one said, spraying his face with spit.

He wanted to make himself small, to crawl across the carpet and out the door where he could run to wherever he needed. Their laughs were now being kicked and lobbed like a rugby ball in a ruck, him being mauled in the centre.

"Hiss boy!" one cried, desperate for the name to catch. There were few greater accomplishments within the boarding school environment than labelling a guy with a scarring nickname.

"Haha, Hiss Boy!" A few others laughed, merely following without question as they often did.

"Thsss, thsss, Snake Boy," another screamed, the boy being broken into several syllables as he laughed at his own genius.

"Snake! Snake!" They began chanting with their rough and breaking voices. Mostly, they still sounded like children, but sprinkled amongst them were the growls and savagery of the pubescent male. From then on they'd only call him The Snake.

The hall shook into silence, as the headmaster walked to the top of the room. He was a big lump of a guy, flesh packed tightly into his jersey. His neck was thick and when he turned it, his whole body would follow. Rarely were teachers present at tea, and if they did it was for little more than a passing glance to satisfy administration or ensure that meals were eaten in a timely manner. It was rare for the boys to not scoff their food before the teachers had even sat down and much of meal time was wasted with banter or bullying.

"Good evening, gentlemen," he said, as the boys looked around smirking at the formality. His mouth was wide as he invited an extra rounded arrogance to his vowels, slow and proud. "As we all know, Lourdston College has long been an esteemed and reputed establishment known not only to make men of boys but to make great leaders of men. Through our halls, we've witnessed several of our nation's greatest diplomats and ministers blossom under our firm hand and inspirational guidance." The boys began to shuffle in their seats as the possibility of a long lecture rose like muck in a pond.

"We have had the greatest privilege of any school in this glorious country of ours, and that is to have stood beside future kings, dine with them, drinking from the spring of wisdom, and to hunt with them as they grew from princes to crown." He took a pause, as though he campaigned for the boy's investment and awe. They were not easily inspired, least not at supper when the formalities could slide under the bed and girly books could be plucked from trunks and cases.

"This evening, we were welcomed with the news that our own great king found the tutelage at the palace to no longer suffice when it came to the training of his own sons, and that it is, in the reputation of kings before him, that Lourdston

College be the most suitable school for the princes to step into their marvellous destiny."

A collective whoosh of air flooded from noses as the boys signalled humour without committing to a laugh, which would under these circumstances reap swift punishment or expulsion. Legend of the boys and their mother's mollycoddling had wafted through the city and into boarding school language. They'd been through no less than three schools as they pranced their polished boots across the privileges of royalty. Boarding schools, especially those of boys, were not known to conform to social hierarchies. It was the biggest, then the loudest, and then the roughest that would reign in the dining hall. Often, toward the final year of lessons, the smartest may begin to rise in standing, as the boys became aware of the need for a friend in higher places and women would gush for the man with the clever words.

"The boys have personally requested that we pay absolutely no mind to their status, and the formal addresses that one would require outside of this institution. Here, they are our peers, our chums, our teammates and hunting allies. Now, if you will all join me in the spirit of brotherhood, as we welcome our two newest pupils at Lourdston." The headmaster began tapping on the table that stood before him, his hand beating softly while those around him pounded and grunted in a display of erupting masculinity.

The princes walked in, their legs dropping from their waistbands like young girls at a recital. Slender and delicate, their faces shaped in the intimate cup of a mother's hand, as though she'd cupped them there since birth.

"Boys." The headmaster gestured, as though awaiting a regal speech or introduction. Instead, the princes floated lily hands to their faces, fingers wriggling as though to wave. Perhaps in the palace that had been considered sweet.

The headmaster, who always had words, suddenly fell silent. His face was struck with dread for his task ahead. He nodded to the princes, holding an arm behind them to guide them out. Their eyes gaped like the lips of fish being pulled by a bloodied hook. They looked terrified and rightly so. The halls here were old and falling, wood raw and not adorned with the pigments and flourishes in the palace or even the schools in the city. It was cold in the north and the windows were not dressed to shield the stabbing night. There was no carpet, and outside the pomp, there would be no warmth.

It was like a meat auction, thought The Snake, skating the line of pitying the poor boys while also welcoming the reprieve from his own misery. He was grateful for the distraction, for whatever was due to be dished to him that evening would now play second fiddle, or third, to these two lambs walking to slaughter.

He wondered how long they'd last, if this were their terminus, a final 'breaking in' like a horse. Lourdston was so far from the city, and The Queen would never have to know of the beatings and labour that'd serve as initiation.

The King slung his own reputation around his offspring. There'd been many, it was well known, but they were all bastards and even the beefiest could not be claimed in the court as being of regal birth. The King looked at his slippery and salved 'princes' and welcomed the duty of hardening them. His wife had too long promised that manhood would erupt organically, yet their bodies only pressed into the shape of tall girls.

"Dear boys," the headmaster continued, this time less diligently and without the duty of infecting a future king with the Lourdston brand of inspiration, "as you know, the policy at Lourdston is such that in each year we have very minimal places to offer. As this year has seen many of your fathers' lives taken by the horrors of war, our rooms have swelled and we filled that capacity much earlier than during peace times. As the placement of the princes is a matter of national security, these boys will require their private rooms, so those four boys who have most recently joined us must now share a room."

A few murmurs scuttled across the dining hall. "I thought they wanted to be treated like everyone else," someone said loud enough to be heard but without the range to be detected.

"It'd do you well to remember your privilege," said the headmaster, again slow and plummy. "We are fortunate to have access to such space here, no other school has single rooms for lodging." He peered down his nose at the boys, his head high and neck arching in a stern warning. Whinge. His stance implored the boys. Complain. He urged them with his shrivelled mouth puckered in disdain, eager to punish any tantrum.

The Snake's cheeks stung scarlet, his eyes panning the room

before looking down and taking the bed behind the door. The boy, if you could call him that, had moved to the side of the room which seemed to accommodate him much better. The floors stretched a couple of metres longer and there was a cupboard at his feet. The Snake slid his boxes under his bed, realising the headboard would mostly serve as a doorstop.

The Snake was intimate with his new roommate, well at least his fist. He knew its smell best, like grass and gravy, and the lingering smell of hard soap. He remembered it striking him, not long after they'd revealed him not to be a murderer, but a mute. He knew how it looked when held to the sky, boys cheering him, The Snake's blood trickling between scarred knuckles.

He sat on the mattress edge, thought after thought after thought crashing into his brain. He needed a strategy, he thought, yet knew that those had rarely served him. He needed an alliance, or protection, or some way to find a room for himself or another college.

He'd never been in such forced quarters with another before. At home, it was just him and his sister and they'd each had their own room until she fell ill and then it was just him while his parents were at work. He wasn't sure how to be, or what to do. How to avoid the beating when differing points of view would square upon another.

The others, too, would now have access to him. He couldn't lock the door as he pleased anymore. He watched the boy making his bed across the room, following the exact protocol instructed by the dorm master. There was something obtuse and clumsy about the way he did it. His hands pressed the corners flat, but chubby fingers would roll and curve without the angular creases that would crisp beneath other's hands.

The boy fell onto his bed, his body bouncing and squeaking the old, lax springs. His eyes shot to the ceiling above him for a few moments, as though he too, sought a strategy.

If I could find something quiet, perhaps he'd never notice me. I could be important and busy and never see a reason to question the boy or scrape against his comfort. I could read and bury myself, and never so much as glance his way. The boy looked quite the man. Surely after summer, he would move on and once more The Snake could be alone.

He wondered too if maybe he should talk. A relaxed 'hey' and nod in his direction. To level the playing field and render them brothers. But even if he wanted, his mouth would curl and his tongue would flick as worry invaded his thoughts. He knew he thought too much. Sometimes, when he didn't think, a perfect 'hello' would roll from his mouth. It was always easier with his sister's friends; they'd never castrate him if he slurred or mispronounced a word or sprayed them as his tongue snapped over saliva.

He watched the boy clenching his fists as he stretched his arms, maybe weary, maybe in preparation for beating. He couldn't try talking now, even if it were a reasonable tactic.

The Snake pulled the box from beside his bed, dragging it slowly as the soft hush of cardboard swept upon an old wool rug. His head was bowed as though looking solely at the box, yet his right eye held the shape of the boy on the bed. He flicked his fingers over books, searching for something busy, something important, not desperate. Chemistry, Blake, Edwin Hubble? There, he thought, 'Conquerors'. If it weren't to be him at least he could live vicariously.

The Snake watched the boy, a slight sliver of his eye cast above the book to confirm the boy's position. It seemed he had already established a status quo. Not talking, not acknowledging him, pretending that the little piss-ant was not in his room. He now lay on his bed, a ruby-shined cricket ball spinning between his fingers as he flicked it to the air and caught it with a slap.

That would hurt, The Snake thought, as though doing an inventory on all the ways this boy could maim him. A huge trophy sat atop a box, shining with decency and respect, that could be taken to his skull cracking it like an egg.

The Snake squashed himself to the wall, trying to make his bed without taking a single inch of the boy's space. He was good at beds, he thought, which was probably not something he'd claim loudly even if he could. That was girl stuff, he knew. Having a gift for the domestic amongst boys was a glaring sin worthy of shaming. Still, he enjoyed the feel of crisp sheets with strong folds, and even on the worst days, he'd look forward to that singular comfort.

Somehow he slept well, which caused him alarm when he opened one eye and saw the boy's bed made, and him not there. He'd intended to stay alert all night, to watch the boy and understand his every move, every twitch, or hear if dreams haunted him. Instead, he'd slept deeply and now the boy was probably corralling the rugby team for a bite of brutality before oats.

He dressed, fumbling with buttons between shaking fingers. He could hide, he thought, although he knew that would barely discourage them. Often they'd wait by the door as classes finished and one after the other would beat him as he walked down the hall.

He drifted down the corridor, expecting the rumblings of a gearing team, amped for battle. His feet moved with such haste, however, that he soon realised the only noise had been coming from leather on linoleum. Step, step, step and the occasional drag as his frightened limbs faltered. The last of the rooms before the stairwell had been his until last night, but now he saw the door wide open and realised it belonged to a prince.

As he wandered closer, he heard an unusual pairing of voices, one a thud, the other a trill. He kept his eyes locked on the stairwell as he walked by, hoping to go unnoticed. From the corner of his eye, he recognised the boy, that same clumsy shape built for murder that lay across from him last night. *Keep walking. Keep walking.*

As he snuck into the mess for breakfast, he saw the boy no longer sitting at his table by the servery. Further back, he sat flanked by the princes. The scene was clunky and looked like pearls on a bull. Each of the princes sat with their mouths agape in wonder, like he was someone grand, someone important. It was the same look of importance that the others used to give him after a beating. His chest seemed broader now, his neck longer, as though their opinion nourished muscle. The boy, it appeared, had promoted himself to royal defence.

Perhaps he's lazy, thought The Snake one day as the summer drew closer. The boy had now stopped playing rugby, and even as the days stretched further into nights, he was neither on the field nor pitch. He'd stopped haunting the corridors with his blow upon his startled face. Without effort now, he could yield the same smack of awe from the princes as he could playing sport or beating.

The boy still would not speak to The Snake, who suffered badly not knowing if the silence tended to respect or contempt. He'd sit on his bed at night, lamp glowing beside him and flickering over the words in his book. He'd try reading but would not let himself become too immersed and loosen the guard he had poorly imagined himself to have.

One night, The Snake feigned reading while the corner of his view was clamped on the boy. He noticed that he'd stopped throwing the cricket ball and had begun watching him read, driving a prickle of hairs up his neck and down his arms. Reading was not a spectator sport, he thought, wondering what on earth this boy could be surveying him for. It was scrutiny, an obvious, probing, scalpel in which his eyes squinted and his mouth all fell to one side, the occasional ripple waving through his cheek as though he was biting or grinding his teeth.

What was he doing? The Snake coiled further in fear. It seemed given the choice of a wolf breathing down his neck and poring over his routine, The Snake was torn. There was some strange comfort in knowing what was coming, be it fist or foot.

The boy sat up, and The Snake lit every one of his nerves as a fire signal to the next. His face burned and even in the poor light of the lantern, he was certain his weakness shone bright. He knew what men looked like when rage boiled within. Hands clenching and knuckles white, pulsing and pumping the blood as they draw fuel to their muscles. The savage lines of tendons that would stretch from knuckle to wrist, then upward to forearms that bulged with beef and might.

The Snake sunk further into his bed, further into his words, as the boy stood all thick and clumsy. He took a few steps, each thud heavy upon floorboard then rug, and then a pause, as though to question himself. Again, more steps, until he reached The Snake's bed, plucking the book between his fingers.

"What is this?"

"I-i-i-i-important," was all The Snake could muster. His strategy remained, and for the past few weeks it had seemed to work. If he could seem busy, seem important, maybe he'd be spared.

"The same one." The Snake still sat with 'Conquerors'. He'd not dared draw attention to himself by switching to a different book. 'Conquerors' had thus far served him well, and while amongst his favourites, he was certain William Blake would guarantee a beating.

"I-i-impor-tant."

Something in the boy's eyes combusted like he'd stopped

seeing a useless thing and now found himself a treasure. The Snake shifted, uncomfortable. He'd never been looked at with those eyes before.

"Read!"

The boy seemed excited now, as though something in the way The Snake had stammered softened him, relaxed him and settled the beast that had seconds before thumped across the dorm. He sat, next to The Snake. His solid body plonked down on the bed with springs startling and squeaking at the intrusion. His thick neck stretched graceless over The Snake's shoulder, a fat crane scanning the text.

The Snake froze. *Not that,* he thought, almost preferring the belting he thought he'd get. It was excruciating, to be stuck in that moment, someone listening to him stutter and spit and words swirl between tongue and tooth and only half to be birthed, the rest sticking to his throat like tar or lava.

"I-I-I-I-I ca-ca-can't," said The Snake, wondering what would be worse, the fist or the fall of broken words.

"Read!"

"I-i-i-i-it woul would would b-be th-th-th-th—" His tongue slid again like a snake, and he recoiled, waiting for beating, or mockery or anything but what the boy was actually giving, which seemed just short of elation. His eyes sparkling and twinkled with the lamplight, were they misting with glee? The boy nodded, pointing back to the book for The Snake to continue.

The Snake looked back at his words, they used to be his refuge but now he stood naked and desperate to honour them as they deserved. "It woul-would be th-the the g-lory o-o-of Alexander." Words slid into another, and the boy watched on beaming. His chubby fingers moved like sausages to grab The Snake's hand and began tracing the words as a mother would to a child.

He can't read, The Snake realised, his fingers relaxing as the boy took his hand back and once again watched. This time, his stutter being gilded with the letters on the page. Every time his tongue would buckle or curl or fall to the wrong side, he'd point longer and harder at each letter, emphasising its sound.

"I-i-i-i-it—" the boy started, his finger tracing the 'I' and 't' with desperate specificity. "It wou-woul-would be—" His mouth calling the letters to find a space in his memory.

But they love him. The Snake thought to the way they cheered for the boy on the field and off. The way they'd call his name over and over and over as he ran, knocking men piece by piece like pawns on a chessboard. *They love him and they loathe me.*

He dropped his head further, to his pillow now. The scratch of wool blanket rubbing at his cheek. The lantern casting shadows of this man, the man they'd call a boy though he'd not been for many years, and the dark impression of pages turning and a leg piling atop another.

He'd only ever witnessed brotherhood from the outside. Although he'd longed deeply, he saw the other boys as a force much broader than himself, that he could never slide amongst them unnoticed. He'd tried to perfect his words, practice them in his solitude, so that when the moment arose he too, could make them laugh. In all the times of forcing himself to like them, he never imagined that it could be easy. That there could be another way.

Yet here he sat, legs outstretched on his bed, the boy's knee resting upon his own. Here he sat, flaws naked to the cold air and dancing like Mata Hari by flame at night. With each new paragraph, he'd lean in closer, fingers gliding as words spat wildly. He never imagined that through the violence of his tongue, clunking and slapping against his palate as the words would skew and spray, he could offer more of himself, the threads binding them in brotherhood.

He thought of the boy when he first approached his bed. His fist gnarled and shining like the moon plastered in the clear winter night. His lips curled and he bit his cheek. It was violence, of course, but now The Snake saw more. Like the stars, crashing and colliding, longing to be bound tighter in gravity. He too, blindly sought connection.

THE GREATEST SHOW ON EARTH

The Trapeze Artist held her arms wide beside her, fingers splayed to the audience below, and she straightened her spine like a cobra stretching to its charmer. Her eyes had been bound tight by the silky blindfold, although she knew the space all too well. The smells, of horse and cracked leather whips, of lion and bear. The drop before her hummed with a vacuous symphony, empty and hollow to sound. To her side, another drop, this one whooshing with the murmurs and whispers of a crowd seeded with deep anticipation.

They'd heard of her, this acrobat from France. While the others were only known to the crowd by their titles, like 'clown' or 'lion tamer' or 'horse rider,' her name shone electric on posters. *Équilibre.* Barely a mouth could speak the tongue in London, yet their eyes would spark and shine when it was said.

There'd been a great ruckus when the rumours started gathering steam that the French circus had been courted by no less than The Queen. She'd heard of their magic and held such entertainment in the most regal of banners, believing the marriage of art and physical mastery to be an inspiration to her countrymen. The Queen sat, on several occasions now, visiting with dignitaries and ambassadors. She'd brought her mother once, who seemed not to forget the great hatred that coursed between their countries. She found the French to be vulgar and reminded her spirited daughter of the necessities for composure. One wouldn't wish to be seen as weak, smiling or surprised by the antics of a 'flying Gypsy'.

The Queen did not attend on this night, and the crowds were flushed with the waft of spoiled food and mucky boots. The stench, Équilibre thought, was not unlike that of the animal carriages, thick and primitive. The Queen had, in a show of her hand, dealt compassion to her hungry subjects. After she'd had her own child, she tended to be more thoughtful toward their needs, imploring the government to provide measures for the worsening crime and poverty. On this night, she gifted them entry to the circus, a reprieve from their putrid lives.

Équilibre held her shoulders back, her body wrapped in cloth so tight and so luminous that it seemed to glow without even the gas lanterns casting their light upon it. Purples, pinks, and golds all swirled from décolletage to ankle, with a flounce of silk resting on her hips. Her hair was tight, drawing upon her brow and framing the porcelain face and ruby stained lips. When she'd wrapped the blindfold around her eyes, they'd all gasped, suitably primed by the whispers of those who'd attended in the days before.

Much of her success, she believed, was due to those eager crowds that would burst and rupture with wonder and bewilderment. They'd watch her soar thirty feet into the sky, their mouths gaping wide and necks craning to look as though a comet burned the night sky. Their faces would light and spark in glee, and the logistics became unfathomable to them. Had it been thirty or forty feet? Stories tended to bounce ever higher. Once it was heard that she was 'at least fifty-feet high', which although untrue was quite possible. To her, it was the physical demands that were the hardest, not the heights. But most of the audiences had barely visited a third-storey apartment, let alone swung from a bar tethered to a tent pole.

She wondered sometimes if they would even notice her if she performed the same show at five or ten feet. There was something in the inconvenience, she thought. That they had to crook their necks and fix their eyes in the same way they'd gaze upon heavens at night. That angle of sight reserved for stars and luminaries and the passing clouds unfurling and flashing the promise of blue.

A new emptiness fell before her, and she recognised it as the collective gasp as The Ringmaster climbed the ladder behind her. She knew what he'd be doing. His hand and mouth, as though controlled by the one, singular muscle, both gesturing a bright idea with the flick of an index finger and his lips rounding. It was almost like he'd ingested the thought like a slurp of thick soup from a spoon. His eyes would grow wild, the rehearsed spontaneity popping from him to the audience, each of them flickering with the same excitement.

He'd draw his finger to his lips, with the other pointing up, having them invest in a betrayal of Équilibre. There seemed something powerful in the way he could manipulate them, these poor and bedraggled urchins and the way they were eager to play a part in whatever fate would be brought upon the greatest trapeze artist alive. They become the masters, the puppeteers for the marionette as she hung from her wires.

She'd stand stroking the bars and rope as if to test its strength and prove her professionalism. In fact, she would do this in the hours before the crowds would arrive, yet it would be more brutish, more forceful and without the grace she showed now, each hand synchronised in more of a mime of what it could look like if the bar was no more than five feet high.

She'd feel the last few heaves on the ladder. He wasn't a huge man but his size had prevented him from climbing such a ladder before his ego implored him so. As she felt his boots tiptoe onto the platform, her hands would swan and glide, as though in readiness for her grand dive. Her neck would arch and face the roof, she'd seat herself upon the bar like a girl on a swing and in the most elegant of stretches, she'd bring her hands high above her, and then down behind her back, expanding her chest in a final flourish of preparation.

Here, he'd snare her. He'd again place his finger to mouth, the crowd now mystified and too far in to give up his rouse. He'd pull a cloth from his pocket, whipping it into a long length of ribbon, and tie her hands behind her. She'd gasp, rocking her shoulders from side to side while sitting tightly on the high bar.

She wasn't gifted like he when it came to mime. She

wriggled and writhed, her shoulders too expressive, her neck not enough so. Behind the blindfold, her eyes fixed on the precise timing The Ringmaster had given her—the third bell from the tower—that they'd never hear as their senses were primed for the visual. She'd know the moment anyway, as the crowd tended to give themselves away with a collective gasp when The Ringmaster would smile wide. His moustache framed the curves of his mouth, his finger in one final flourish of genius as he'd point, and mostly they'd nod, although the timid would cover their mouths and cower before he pushed her from her perch.

When she moved to France they'd been so taken by her precision that rounding her in the theatre proved mostly a waste of time. She was the girl from the east, who every day trained and pushed her body further. Her body could move like no other, her dedication to the profession soared beyond all that had come before her. She'd been on a bar since before she could walk, getting better and more technical was all that drove her.

She'd recognised it in The Queen too. The stern face she kept with the senators and diplomats when even the clown summoned laughter from all around her, she sat, her gaze steely and hard. She'd been trained well to hold herself together. Her advisor's lips would stiffen when the crowd would erupt, they'd not the regal blood to harness amusement—it would still register on their faces even without a smile.

And then, there was the night when The Queen came

alone, with just two of her closest ladies. Her cheeks were fuller, flushed, and her eyes sparkling brighter than she'd ever seen them, even with The Prince. She was just a girl again. Her hair fell loose and her dress yielded to her breath. She was quite the different woman, Équilibre noted.

Équilibre's face was never soft or warm like The Queen's. Her eastern angles were hard and spiteful, her jaw would show the bite of sacrifice that she'd developed over years of training. Her lips would draw narrow in their seams, a telling tribute to gathering composure. It had been taught to her that if her mouth were to move she could show the grip of fear. And if her mouth showed it, her body believed it. If she gasped or was stunned, then she would fall. Mastery would be the key to her glory.

As she gripped the bar and leapt from the platform, her legs piked and swinging above her, locking her to the bar just moments after her fingers had released. It was a standard move for her, it surprised her that crowds had not come to expect it after so long, and yet every time there'd be the moment of pregnant silence, when they'd inhale desperately, fearing a fall.

This night, such a sound did whip the air, a solitary gasp feminine and squeaking. The shriek gave way to a relieved giggle and another quickly joined it. A third, this one more breathy and thicker, definitely royal, she thought, then too joined the chorus.

It was The Queen, Équilibre thought, the slamming point of intimacy distracting her momentarily. All that she'd heard, all that she'd known, was that royals were to hold emotion on their tongue and never let it slip. But here she was, her laughter almost messy, cackling beneath the bar.

It'd be on Équilibre's mind for a month, the overt display of character and humanity. Of why it was so pertinent to the empire that she never let such sparks fly, weighing inside her, encased with duty. She remembered how it felt when she landed, feeling as though she were the audience, not The Queen sitting. How her heart had fluttered and felt like a hummingbird collecting nectar in her chest. When she returned to her dressing room, there was something brighter, lighter, looking back at her when she looked in the mirror. The hard angles replaced with a softness, the thick powdered skin now shining luminous as though gas lanterns had been set directed at only her.

The night stained her. The innocence, the unbridled joy and brimming giggles would play night after night as she'd stand on the platform. It was not The Queen that she saw, but now the faces of hundreds each popping like a bottle of champagne, their smiles wide and soaked in wonder. It had been the same with The Queen, not just applause for her inhuman skills, but for the experience, the moment, they'd prod and poke at each other desperate to capture the act together.

They were sharing. Their faces hiding no stories, their bodies fluid and flooding with the cascade of emotion that would rise with each act. She began watching them, scrutinising them beyond their wild faces. It wasn't the applause nor the gasps that would grab her now, but the tiny gestures between. The fist clutching at the jacket beside it, hands being held and knuckles white as she'd reach for her blindfold, eyes locking in a conversation richer than words as they'd confess they thought she'd fall and then the ultimate surprise when her ankle clasped the bar.

All this time, she'd thought that she was the magic. Not in an idealistic way or in any hierarchical expression, but in the same way that the finest chef could cook haute cuisine, or the devoted farmer could harvest the sweetest plums. She thought she was the star, and yet now it all seemed null if their experience was tedious.

What if they came alone? She thought one night, as the pine of loneliness sunk once more into her body. Surely, she thought, they'd need friends or family to be with them, for them to hold that intimacy and understand the wordless gestures. She scanned the audience from behind the curtain, watching them move in waves, big and small, some heaving with up to twenty people squeezing together, and then the dribble of the single man finding his seat. She'd watch these single men, expecting them to be silent and with eyes only for her.

And yet here they'd sit, gentlemen even, arms wide open to the pauper next door, laughing and pounding on the skinny frames of those they'd never see outside of the tent. The experience seemed an equaliser, or more, a connector.

She'd watch them leave the big top, their eyes catching friends and strangers alike, eyes wide and faces melting together, as though fused by the shared experience. Despite their differing worlds in the gutter or the glitz, they'd become family here.

She ached deeply for this. Her closest friend had been her teacher, as he'd perfected her attitude and movement. He'd never been tender, always strict and himself devoted only to the craft, but he'd seen her fall many times and never scolded her for it. There had been Viktor for a time, he'd been her partner in the early days when The Ringmaster followed convention. They'd trained together and would sometimes talk outside of training. He'd ask her questions about her favourite acts or her favourite animals or costume. She'd never been asked preferences before, everything had been to satisfy the crowds, so she'd answered him "The Lion Tamer" because of the way the crowd would roar, even though the horse riders would hold her heart and breath still.

When The Ringmaster would finally push her, her balance would be off and gravity would spill her from the bar. She knew what the crowd would be doing, their hands grasping the seat or knees, as though they could control her hands to grab the bar. The air would be sucked from the tent, as every person there would gasp in synchronicity for fear that she would fall.

Her hands, knowing only the bar, would claw to hold on as her body dropped like a hammer to the wood. Her arms stretched above her head, and she would swing into a somersault landing her once again atop the bar. The rest of her show would be performed hands bound and eyes blinded, yet still, the audience's faces would shine, their mouths agape in awe for what her body could do.

When her feet finally rested again on the wooden platform, the arches high and toes splayed in a way that would arch her back too, her chest would rise and fall, exaggerated as she gathered her breath. The Ringmaster would come to unbind her hands, and she would bow as she did every night, one arm to the sky that would pull off her blindfold and lead her head like an invisible string, rising that too to the sky, and then for the arm to guide her upper body to fold forward. Her mouth would stay stuck in the same professional pout.

Instead, this night as The Ringmaster untied her hands, she waved to the crowds as she'd seen The Queen do when she'd ride in her carriage. It was awkward and ungraceful, her hands like chickens being chased by a fox, darting this way and that, lingering for a bit before moving again in another direction. But she heard it, children and women and their breath being stolen by the excitement of this ripe new act.

"She's waving," their voices whispering and then breaking with a wave of elation.

Équilibre pulled at her blindfold, seeing for the first time hundreds of eyes floating beyond faces, giddied and struck by the invitation to connect. They all looked, not applauding this time, but celebrating, cheering together as they raised her to the same.

Her skin pricked with the rising wave of hair standing to attention. Slowly, her mouth peeled back to show white teeth gleaming against ruby stained lips.

They jumped, in a way that had her jump too. It wasn't for fear or fright, but this time their bodies were overwhelmed by the ecstasy of Équilibre seeing them. And not just seeing them, but smiling too, as if she were happy, as if what they did could please her. They cheered higher and higher, their calls and whistles and screams all delighting as she'd turn and bow not to the canvas roof as she had before, but to each person, their eyes locking and her head bowing.

They cheered, celebrated. As did she. Their applause not merely for the artist that flew so far above, but for her, the woman, the tangled emotions and heart pining alone. For the first time, they saw her—instead of awe, there was connection. Not applause, but celebration. A perfect union.

This was gratitude in action. This, for her, was joy.

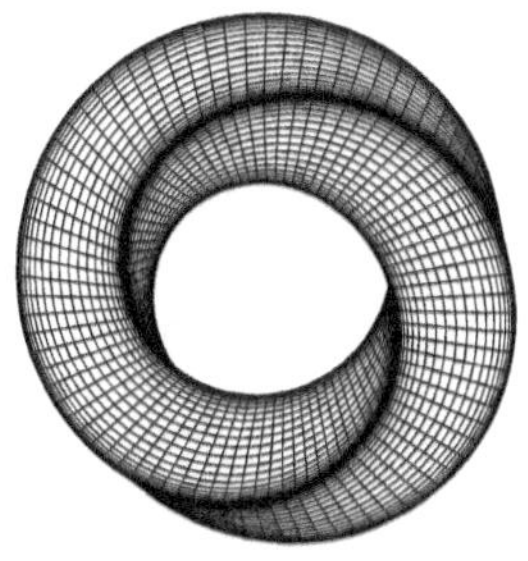

EPILOGUE

"I'm a wizard," the street urchin squealed, her eyes and mouth wide like dishpans as she watched the ball fall back to the ground.

"You mean a witch," The Artist said. It seemed a command as it fell from his mouth, but she barely seemed to consider it.

"No, a wizard!" She corrected him, and he supposed that for a child so young, and for a girl indeed, it was no ill of her vocabulary. Witches were for the most part viewed as evil, while wizards were revered and celebrated in myth and legend alike.

She threw the ball again, this time higher, her eyes sparkling with the glint of the overhead sun. It was a warm day, he felt it this time when he painted her. It wasn't him making it a warm day, it just was. There was grass, not lush and thick as he'd painted before, but tender new shoots growing against frostbitten earth. She didn't stand on the grass, it would have been so much more poetic for him to paint her this way, but she wouldn't. She liked the sound the ball made as it hit the cobblestones hard after she'd thrown it so high. To her, it would make the ball sound the way she felt, like it had been amongst the stars.

He'd seen her, the real her, playing in the Centro with the other urchins, and often marvelled at her bewilderment as she tossed anything skyward. The ball, the cloth, the shoe or coin, they'd each lead her eye to the heavens where her gaze would greet creation. "You like your ball, eh?" he asked her, feeling somewhat proud to have gifted her this.

"Yes," she said in a way that almost disappointed The Artist. It wasn't because it was a ball, he thought, this perfectly round thing, ripe for bouncing and tossing and catching and games. It wasn't because there was anything more remarkable about this thing than any other thing she would play with. She said 'yes' because she did enjoy throwing things. And on this canvas, there were few things to throw.

"Do you miss your friends?" This time he asked her more sternly, forcing her to hold the ball as she responded to his tone.

"Sometimes," she said after considering it for a while. She threw the ball again before adding, "you know, sometimes I didn't live with them. And sometimes, I did."

He wondered what she meant; if it were her on the canvas talking or the real street urchin from the Centro. He searched her words for clues, not knowing how to ask a pool of paint if she meant in her real life, or here, where she was just fantasy. *I didn't … I did.* The way she described it as though it were the past, and not her life now, with him and the brush. "Where else did you live?" he asked, hoping she'd privy him to the life she lived sometimes.

"I had a family," her mouth widened as the words fell, as though she'd found some elusive loophole within the constraints of society. She giggled like any other child would if their hiding spot playing seek had been discovered.

"You had a family?" He leaned in, twisting his brush into the white to catch the glint in her eye.

"My mama died, but papa was a baker. My brother worked with him." This time, her voice was lower, and the way she smiled felt like it was for him, not her. Like he needed the comfort to hear of heartache in a child, yet she was comfortable with the pain.

"My mama died too," The Artist said, his voice lowering also. She smiled back at him, that same smile that offered him the comfort she'd long ago come to find within.

It'd been a strange conversation, this one more than the others. He'd come to her canvas with the same arrogance that would accompany age, and yet for her, he had so many questions. He assumed he'd known her from what he'd seen, and that she'd answer as he expected, but as the ground began to form beneath her, and the sky shone deep in blue, a church appeared in the distance. Her answers began to digress, departing from what he wanted and what he knew.

She took him beyond the Centro, to a church that stood

many years ago, that he remembered from his youth. He'd been locked there once, he remembered, as the gardener tended to shrubs and hadn't seen him in there. They'd begun locking the gates after the raids but The Artist was just a little boy and intended no harm. He'd stood at the altar and in his squeaking voice started to give a sermon.

Why she led him there, he did not understand, but the church was miles away and he wondered if she really knew it, or by now perhaps he'd gone mad and his mind was playing tricks. He'd been so wrapped up in the painting of his series, he barely remembered the artist he was when he'd paint by prescription.

The bells would ring as she'd throw her ball, birds warbling in the distant pines, the sky heavy and warm. It was so specific to this little girl, he thought, the details each dictated by her, her smile the gauge of its authenticity. But he couldn't help but feel himself swimming in there, as though gravity didn't exist. Even without such a static law as gravity, her world felt real. More than real, as though the details in his life outside the studio were contrived but this was organic.

One day, he sat with her and asked her about joy. "How is it that you and the other urchins can shine so brightly?" She beamed, as though he'd finally stumbled on a topic that could capture her.

"To know how they shine, you need to know how they ache," she answered, her words timid and slow like a child with little grasp of language but stabbed with the understanding of a crone.

"And how do they ache?" he asked, assuming the poverty and violence on the streets to be the extent.

"When one dies, they take his hair to the fountain and wash it with the soap where women have washed their linen. Then, they take it to the wigmaker and each will get a coin." He remembered the coughs, the hacking phlegm and bile as they'd cause themselves to vomit from their spasming lungs.

His face dropped. Not much could have described their ache so fully, their desperation so heavily. That she'd picked this moment in time, not the everyday jostling for crumbs of bread or the sentries that would hit them with batons at night in the street, screamed to him that he knew little of aches and less of children.

She told him of the day the littlest had died. This one had barely been walking and its brother had to tend to its nappies. It had never been well, but when it died the brother had wailed like an ox in castration. A deep, bellow beyond the vessels of his lungs. He'd cried for days and then one day stopped. His eyes were so swollen that they'd near fused together, his cheeks like beets shining with the glaze of tears and snot wiped aside. He'd walked that night to see the broken volcano, it no longer boiled but it would still shield from the morning sun. As it broke, its rays would beam down on him and his breath became settled. The tourists were kinder here, and it was still early enough for the sentries to not shunt him away with their batons or poles. One tourist, a man, saw him sitting with his eyes hollowed and hurt. He leaned over, holding out a hand clutching something inside. The boy saw a glint of silver and opened his own hand beneath it.

"Time for a change," the man said, a smug grin crawling onto his face as he dropped a wind-up watch into the boy's hand.

"That was the best day of his life," said the urchin, adding, "holding pain and joy together can sometimes feel like heaven." Again, her years seemed to defy her.

She told him of better times too, of the summer when feasts would spill onto the Centro and goat and cheese and olives and tomatoes would be filled beyond the borders of bowls, and nobody would smack at the tiny hands that grabbed all they could. How their games with stick and rock could wind on for weeks before everyone would finish, and the winner would wait on the final days, his score front of mind, counting all others as they finished their go.

It seemed to The Artist that their lives were very much similar to the children of the court except for the brutality.

"Surely," he asked her, "agony is not the only way to joy?" The lines on his face ticked through his thoughts, his memories of his own seedy past also etched with moments of bliss.

"No," she assured, "which is why I only sometimes live there."

He'd wondered what it would mean for a child to make such a choice. She could be four or five, no more than six, and yet here she stood, ball in hand, teaching him of life.

"How did you come to choose?" he asked her, thinking to himself as a four-year-old, or even a twenty-four-year-old, and his capacity to make such wise decisions.

Her little voice flickered like a sparrow in the rain, giggling and weightless. "You know I'm just a painting," she said to him, her voice now light with the nonchalance of a girl with no consequences. "You're painting only what you want to know".

He felt mocked, like she'd reeled him in and then stung him with no higher insights. She threw her ball again and again, each time higher than the last, until she stood holding it under her arm and cupped her hand to her hip.

"You know, if you painted anyone only to ask them one thing, they'd know it well too." Her voice was whiny like the children of the court when their mothers told them 'no more cake and they say that they were a duke and they'd tell papa. She put the ball down, more in defiance than boredom. As a protest to his gift of arrogance.

She sat now, her back to him and her feet in the dirt. Sun hadn't touched the shoots of grass here yet, the pine stood tall between it and the sky, and it would be a few more weeks until the sun would rise high enough for sprouts to emerge. He wondered what she was doing, her dress getting muddy on the sides where ice had melted into the tree roots. She wouldn't answer him, all those moments where he'd thought of her to be wise beyond years, now ridiculed him as he sat watching a tantrum.

He watched her elbow moving, sharp and swift and then swirling around. He recognised the movement but not in this context. It was deeply familiar to him, the passion and fury, the calm and carving. He squinted his eyes to remove his girl as the subject and focused only on the arm. It was an artist, he realised, all those years teaching at the court and watching novice and expert sit with their backs to him while they'd sketch wildly with their elbows flailing. She fit snugly amongst the experts, which hardly surprised him. She was right, he only painted what he wanted to know.

He tried to glimpse over her shoulder, but she'd move to stop him like the urchins would guard their bread. They moved like rats, or faster, heads following shoulders and sometimes shoulders following heads, depending on who wanted their food.

"What are you doing?" he asked, his voice now soft and loaded with deference. He had only painted what he wanted to know, but now he knew there was more he needed to know. It wasn't all fitting snugly into his notion of understanding as he thought it would. There was indeed greater mystery within.

"Drawing," she said. Her voice was cool and simple, as any other four-year-old with a pencil would say it. Matter-of-fact, nothing important.

But it was important and he knew it.

"What are you drawing?" Again, his voice pandering to her temperament, not wanting to probe her for specifics like before, not wanting her to answer in his way, but wanting her to tell him what it meant.

"A picture." Again, her voice was simple, although maybe this time you could almost call it singing, it had sweetened.

"What's in your picture?" He asked, her back still turned

and no apparent indication that she intended to face him.

"I'm a wizard," her voice, again so sweet and lulling him with the delicate trill of a four-year-old.

"Oh, a witch," he said it again, remembering their conversation before. He'd realised as it finished dripping from his tongue that witches were seen as evil these days and searched for a better feminine word.

"No!" Her tantrum returned. "A wizard!" Her voice was now coarse as though she'd been crying a while or held in her throat some gravel. She sounded older, much older, like a woman that lived in the mountains and spent her time herding goats.

"What's the wizard doing?" He asked, investing in her story enough to calm her outburst.

"Drowning," she said, her voice again sweet yet tinged with the slightest tone of play, like a cat with a string.

He felt her tugging at him, and his thoughts spun to a man standing on the stern, the face of a storm staring him down while he called and laughed and beat at his chest in maniacal defiance. His eyes lit with the wild beauty of joy, of the moments before death would ring his knell and life was streaming undiluted. No thoughts of navigation or wages or ports and payment. The blood in his veins coursing with adrenaline and spirit and submission to the gods.

"Anything else?" He asked her again, her tiny life now spanning the voice of muse, as her words slammed him with a vision ripe for his masterpiece.

"A girl in a prison, but it's a whole world" her eyes seemed to not comprehend this one, she'd look at it as though trying to make sense. "It's not here now, it's another now".

The Artist sat back, his fingers fizzing like the air before thunder, and his heart charged an extra beat as he witnessed art beyond himself.

"That's why I choose," she said, breaking his frenzied thoughts as he let each word sink in.

"That's why you choose what?" he asked, his whole body now pumping and bursting with new neural connections.

"That's why I choose to live with the urchins," she answered. She turned to him now and her head fell to the side, her chubby little face reminding him of his question before.

"Oh! Yes, why you choose to live with the urchins," he replied, his words loud and festive, as though remembering the question alone would answer it. His mind whirred for a moment before he realised she'd not told him anything. "So, why?"

"Because I'm a wizard!" She said, her little voice choked with the hilarity of him not understanding her. It seemed quite the favour of childhood, she thought, that she could be cryptic and simple at once, as adults would to her when they'd say things like "because that's the way it is."

The Artist sat back, watching her more. Childish games, he thought. The nubile imaginings of youth. It was beautiful and fertile, but it was hardly logical. Her head had returned to her drawings, her elbows again swivelled and swirled. It was that of masters, he thought, the way she'd move her hands.

He'd watched The King and his men each turn to visual arts, and their hands would clunk and pop. She wasn't like that at all.

"Done!" she called out, her hands pressed together in prayer, as she turned to him, her face electric and brimming. "Now, cover your eyes." Her tender voice was the only part of such a command that he complied to. "No peeking."

He heard her tiny feet shuffle, soft skin across the canvas. "Now," she cried, and he opened his eyes to her giddy squeals as she threw the ball to the sky again.

It was beautiful indeed, watching her throw that ball. But under the bracken beside a pond, she'd carved a series of portraits into the dirt with a stick, that held no less potency than the frescos in chapels.

"I'm a wizard," she said, pointing with her stick now and telling the story as every child would returning from school, "and I drowned but after that, I could do magic."

"You mean you were a wizard," he again corrected her, marvelling at her immersion in her stories.

"No, I am a wizard," she said and moved on. "I'm a girl who works in a place, and it's like a jail, but it's a world, and there are carriages that go really fast without horses. And one day I met a boy and he showed me that it wasn't really a prison."

The Artist looked over to the picture she pointed at now. Huge circles beaming like stars on the front of a mechanical carriage. The detail was impeccable.

"I'm a mama," she says proudly, like the little girls in the court would as they held out their dollies. "And my baby is a god." She continued through, pointing and excitedly telling of each painting and her other 'lives'.

As her stick fell to the last one, his eyes froze and his mouth went dry. Something he'd called for had its claws around his throat and needed to be paid. The picture was spectacular, not in the same style as her others, but dutifully, painfully, his. He recognised his agonised strokes as he'd try to paint joy to a face, her face. The way the trees swayed as if in breezes soft and summery, exactly how he would. And somewhere she'd found crocus in the blight of spring and sprinkled saffron in the corner, his name in red.

"I'm an artist," she said, this time less childish and more motherly. His face was pale and he clutched at his chest, feeling surely his heart must be failing. "This is why I choose to go with the urchins," she went on to finish his question. "Because every struggle makes the joy shine brighter. It's only in the dark of night that the moth finds the flame. I choose that like I choose to drown, and I choose to take poppy and choose for my home to burn."

"You are a wizard." The Artist's tongue grappled with the words, though in his mind fragments began to stir and rumble in connection.

"In another now," she said. Her voice cut with a truth that he'd never heard so potent.

"Another now." He repeated, his head nodding and a smile crawled across his face, like that of a child's. The vision of his opus sprawled across his mind, of joy, of what it was and what it wasn't.

His fingers gripped tight around the brush, crimson paint bleeding from bristles as the canvas yearned for his sigil.

Another now. He thought. *Another now.*

ABOUT THE AUTHOR

Eos Azar is an astrologer navigating the deep and mystic fields of pristine alignment, and feels most nourished when yielding herself to the inevitable and exquisite energies of archetype and arc, of consciousness and change.

When not immersed in the energetic realms, Eos loves long holidays in warm destinations. Her soul thrums eternal in Kythera, Greece.

Her digital home EosAzar.com hosts a bounty of magnificent, expansive offerings for seekers and shadow alchemists, including *The Joy Decision: Deeper* – materials for advanced explorations of joy.

To join Eos within her world, scan the QR code and discover yourself in the land of living myth.